Medicine Wheel Trilogy

Advanced Guide

Grandmother Puddingstone

First Edition

PAGE PUBLISHING, INC.
New York, NY

First originally published by Page Publishing, Inc. 2019

ISBN 978-1-64462-809-6 (Paperback)
ISBN 978-1-64462-810-2 (Digital)

Printed in the United States of America

Contents

Preface

Now that you have your medicine wheel in front of you, you are probably wondering how you can add to the wheel. The answer is, yes, you can. In the *Advanced Guide*, I am only adding eight more circles connecting the totems, the rocks or minerals into the wheel. The *advanced medicine wheel* will have three full circles. Your medicine wheel can be used as a tool in guiding you along your life's journey no matter how simple or complicated you choose to make it.

In the *Medicine Wheel Trilogy—Advance Guide,* you will be exploring new views and thoughts that are so outrageous you will be afraid to speak the words out loud. It is my purpose to trigger your genetic memory to bring you out of your "cultural amnesia."

I hope when you look up to the heavens, you will see your ancestors and remember the "Star People." Remember, you are only a visitor here on Mother Earth / Turtle Island, and your home is in the stars.

Chapter One

Spirit Guides

There are two kinds of spirit guides: spiritual and physical. Native American Indian spirit guides can be compared to guardian angels. Some medicine women believe if you do not believe in guardian angels, it is not likely you would not believe in spirit guides.

Spirit guides are not to be confused with your ancestors. Your ancestors will come to you if you call to them or if you are in a situation where they make themselves known. For example, after my father died, he came to my mother in a dream to warn her about the brakes in the car. Another way your ancestors can come to you is through your sense of smell. My friend's grandmother liked to wear lilac perfume. After she died, during my friend's wedding ceremony, she could smell the scent of lilacs and she knew her grandmother was there.

If you don't believe your spirit guide or guardian angel can come to you in a physical form, then let me tell you what happened to my mother during the hurricane of 1938. She was a student at the Henry Lord Junior High School when the hurricane hit the area. When school was dismissed early in the afternoon, my mother and her friend had trouble walking home against sixty- to eighty-mile-an-hour winds. The wind kept blowing them down when a man came out of nowhere and held on to both of them. He led them home safely, but when she turned to thank him, he disappeared.

Spirit guides can also take the form of an animal. Shortly after the husband of my mother's friend died, a German Shepherd was sitting next to her son's car where he worked. He took the dog home to his mother, but she was afraid of the dog because of his size. She came to understand that the dog was there to protect her, and he never left her side. I felt the dog was her husband's spirit protecting her.

Reasons for Spirit Guides

Before you are born, the Creator gives everyone a spirit guide to help them along their path on earth. Your spirit guide is there for you to call on for many reasons; you should let your spirit guide know when you are happy, well, and peaceful. It is good for your spirit guide to know you under positive conditions, because your spirit guide can help you with illness, sadness, and other problems you face in life. You should keep the lines of communication open with your spirit guide.

Your spirit guide is there with you during important and not so important life events. Your spirit guide is always there to help you, whether you realize it or not. You call on your spirit guide at the time of your birth, your marriage, while giving birth or at the time of your death. Some people call on their spirit guides the moment they wake up and just before they go to sleep. Your spirit guide can give you many blessings. A spirit guide can help you recognize and identify unsolved problems. If you ask your spirit guide to help you solve a problem, sometimes the right idea might pop into your head.

Many medicine people use their spirit guide to help them find the right medicine to cure someone. After the medicine person asks their spirit guide to speak with the spirit guide of the person who is ill, the right treatment for the illness can be given. Your spirit guide can guide you to the right person for help with an illness or problem so you can bring your body back to balance state of being. Before you do a sweat or a vision quest, it is necessary to be in communication with your spirit guide. This is because you will come in contact with many different spirits and you can become confused. Your spirit guide is just that, a guide to lead you in the right direction. It is important that you get to know your spirit guide well enough because then you will know if someone is trying to imitate your guide.

Spirit Places

Many people will look for a large old tree or rock to speak with their spirit guide. The tree or rock makes them feel at peace when they leave. Some people have a special place they go to work out their problems and to feel at peace with themselves.

Spirit places can be a mountain, ocean, island, desert, lake, river, valley, or your own bed. The best spirit place is in your mind. Your mind can take you to places where your body cannot go. Many people believe and need a specific building, such as a church or synagogue, as their spiritual place. If you believe this and feel peace, then continue to go there. I know people need a place that is known for being spiritual because they are unable to find one on their own. Remember most of the sacred places in Europe were garbage dumps, barns, or caves. When my parents went to Israel, my father's favorite place was Galilee. It remained untouched. There were no candles, just the sea and the sand where Jesus walked. My father was a religious and good man.

There will be times when you physically cannot go to your spiritual "safe place," this is where your spirit medicine wheel and guide can help you. People who are confined to where they live or work can go to their spirit place to help them get through the day or night.

Have you ever been in a situation where you are so bored listening to a speaker it makes your mind start to wander? Remember how easily your mind floated off to another world and place? That is how easy it is to get to your spirit place. Think where you want to be and be there!

If someone is murdered or assaulted on a sacred place, the act taints the ground. It sometimes can take many years of blessings and prayers to make it sacred again. If someone dies on sacred ground because of natural causes, the ground is not tainted. Sometimes you just have to let Mother Earth heal herself and not let anyone in the area for a long time. Smudging the area helps heal the area.

If you do not know anyone who might help you in locating a sacred spot, the first rule is to look for a high point. The sacred spot will not be at the top but in the middle. Find out which way a lighting storm would hit the hill or mountain, and you will find your sacred spot. On Mount Monanock, one of the sacred spots is off Toll Road on Parker Trail. Instead of going up the mountain, the spot is on your right overlooking the valley. Lightning strikes are common in sacred areas. This applies to a lake or any body of water.

Some people might say, "I don't live near any mountains or the ocean. How can I find a sacred spot?" First, find a local historian to learn the history of the area you live in. Do not ask if they know of a sacred spot, they will think you're crazy. Many sacred spots are hidden in historical places. You have to use your spirit guide to help you find it. The seat at Mount Hope is a sacred place, but historians only recognize it as a meeting place. Old Boy Scout camps are good areas. The Masons and Boy Scouts would pick high-energy places for their boys to spend the summer.

How to Find Your Spirit Guide

If you don't own or like animals, use your clan and totem animals as a starting point to find your spirit guide. Your spirit guide is there to *guide you* on life's journey, so make your choice carefully. Remember how important it is to have a guide throughout your life. Some people would disagree with the idea that you can have more than one spiritual or physical spirit guide. There isn't just one spirit guide but many.

When the Great Creator picked your spirit guide at birth, it may have taken the form of an animal you don't like or are afraid of. My friend was horrified to discover the snake was one of her spirit animals because she was deathly afraid of them. I suggested she research the topic of snakes in order to learn more about them. She read books and articles to overcome her fear of them. Finally, I introduced her to an acquaintance of mine, Lisa, who owned snakes she could touch and hold. She became desensitized to the point that she was able to tolerate them.

For years she had been struggling to lose weight. Since snakes can go for a long period of time without food, she was able to connect with the snake energies of her spirit guide to successfully lose weight.

Many people and organized religions would like to totally eliminate evil or snakes from the world. This is not possible because a spiritual balance would no longer exist. Without bad, there is no good; without darkness, there is no light. How can one differentiate between good and evil unless you have the knowledge of both of them? Snakes are one of the most sacred animals on Turtle Island.

People have different ways of finding their spirit guide. If you are not serious with your intent to find your spirit guide, they will not come to you. Be careful with your thoughts and words when searching for your spirit guide. If someone else is near you, it might be their spirit guide who comes to you. Not everyone gets to meet their guide face to face. The lucky ones do.

There are many different ways to find your spirit guide. First, through meditation. Second, by praying to the Great Creator. Third, by recognizing your spirit guide has already made his or herself known to you. If you were told you had an imaginary friend as a child, it's a good chance the imaginary friend is your spirit guide. If a child believes there is someone there, believe it. Fourth, by going to a place known to be sacred, and fifth, by going to a medicine person.

Meditation is a helpful tool for most people looking for their spirit guide, if you are able to meditate. You can ask your spirit guide to make themselves known to you while you are meditating. Please do not be discouraged if your spirit guide doesn't make themselves known to you on your first try. Don't become angry if you cannot find your spirit guide right away. Your anger will discourage your guide from making him or herself known to you. Some people may never see or find their spirit guide while they are walking Mother Earth. Their spirit guide will come to them at the time of their death. Before people die, they see and talk with their loved ones and their spirit guide.

When you pray to the Great Creator, or God, please be sincere, honest, and humble. The Great Creator gave you your spirit guide before you were born. Pray alone without an audience, it should be you and the Great Creator. Some people need to have someone next to them and be part of a group when they pray. In organized religion, this is a common practice. The Tibetan monks pray in a group, but they have trained themselves to pray as one within the group.

Prayer is as old as time. There are no special words written down for you to memorize and read. Your thoughts and words should come from your heart. When asking to see, hear, speak or touch your spirit guide, be totally open in your mind, body, and spirit.

If someone tells you, you must say their words to find your spirit guide and nothing else works, *run* away as fast as you can. The only set rule in prayer is to be yourself. Only *you* know you and what is in your mind, heart, and soul. Many people, in order to pray, have to go to a known sacred spot. Be careful with this because sometimes what is sacred to someone else may not be sacred to you. Remember to always use a humble tone when calling on your spirit guide. It is better to use your own words, and not someone else's. When calling your spirit guide, follow your heart.

If you go to a "medicine person" who tells you to use their spirit guide to find your own, don't do it. They are trying to manipulate you by using their spirit guide to gain control over you.

Some medicine people can tell you your spirit guide if your spirit guide allows it. They need to ask *your* permission first. There are many people today claiming to be a medicine person and for a price they will tell you your spirit guide. I advise you not to go to these people who ask for money. Most medicine people barter when they offer instructions rather than money.

Sometimes the sacred places have been so overpowered by sadness and horrible events that you can't stay. I return and bring joy and healing to the sacred places whenever I can. Many people forget to go back and thank the Great Creator or whoever helped them. Just don't visit the sacred places when you are sad or troubled; go when you are happy and share your good news and joy.

Last, if you treat your spirit guide as a joke, he or she will not come to you. Respect is everything.

Spirit Wolf Finds a Mate

One evening, Morning Dove was singing to her animal friends by the light of the full moon. Spirit Wolf heard her singing and wanted to know where the beautiful singing was coming from. He followed her voice until he came upon her singing in the moonlight.

At first, he was reluctant to approach her as a wolf because most people fear wolves. She motioned to him to come to her, and held out some berries. He went up to her and laid by her side. He was amazed as she showed *no* fear of him and began to pet the fur on his back. For the first time, he knew love and did not know what to do. When she got up, he followed her to see what village she had come from, then he ran into the woods.

The next day, Spirit Wolf changed back into a man, then he walked into her village. Many of the people of the village followed the laws of his ancestors, but one warrior, Four Feathers, did not. Neither did he have a good heart.

He was chosen to be the mate of the young woman, Morning Dove. He was very jealous of anyone who talked to her. She was a hard-worker and respected by all the people of her village. She had a special love for the forest and all the creatures who lived there. Whenever she was upset or lonely, she would go to the forest. There, the animals would come to her and listen to her singing. The tree would bend their branches to protect her from the rain.

When Spirit Wolf tried to tell Four Feathers he had to pray before a hunt and show respect for the animal he killed, Four Feathers laughed. When he warned him that Spirit Wolf would question him at the next full moon, he laughed even louder. His laughter drew the attention of many of the villagers. The legend of Spirit Wolf was known to all.

When Morning Dove approached Spirit Wolf as a man, she sensed something familiar about him. When she offered him food and a place to stay, Four Feathers became enraged. Evening came, and as she shared a meal with Spirit Wolf, they expressed their love for one another. He told her if he should die as a man, she should lay his body under a pine tree, he would change back into the Spirit Wolf when the moon becomes full again. No human can kill a Spirit Wolf, only the Star People can do it. Whenever he changes from man to Spirit Wolf and Spirit Wolf to man, he always lies down under a pine tree. He told her whenever she walked through the woods, whether day or night, she should look for a pine branch on the ground to carry with her as protection from the Hobomoko. They spent that night as one, and slept in each other's arms.

The next day, Morning Dove did not wake up Four Feathers and bring him his morning meal. Everyone in the wigwam knew he had lost Morning Dove to the stranger. He became enraged and left the wigwam wanting to kill the stranger. He stood outside Morning Dove's *wetu* and waited for the stranger to come out. Inside the wetu, Spirit Wolf told Morning Dove Four Feathers would kill him when he left the *wetu*.

He said, "Remember to lay my body under a pine tree." She nodded her head yes as she watched him leave. When Spirit Wolf crawled out of the *wetu*, he did not see Four Feathers and thought all was good.

Suddenly, without warning, he felt something go through his body and come out of his chest! Four Feathers had pierced his heart with an arrow. Morning Dove came out as Spirit Wolf fell to the ground. He was dead. She screamed and cried over his body. Four Feathers stood there with his arms folded as some of the villages came to comfort Morning Dove. Together, they gently carried the Spirit

Wolf body to a pine tree under the jealous and watchful eyes of Four Feathers. After they laid the body under the pine tree, Morning Dove sat beside him and refused to leave his side. Until the next full moon, some of the villagers brought her food to eat and water to drink. For several days, Four Feathers tried to convince her to leave and come back to the village with him. She would not speak to him. On the last day, Four Feathers told her he was picking another mate.

Evening time, Morning Dove watched as the full moon began to rise. When the moonbeams touched the body of Spirit Wolf, he began to glow in the dark. She watched as his body changed from man to Spirit Wolf. Without saying a word, they both got up and walked through the woods towards the village. When the village people saw them coming, they gathered together and followed them to the center of the village.

Spirit Wolf spoke: "Morning Dove is my mate, and from here on, she will be known as Morning Star." Four Feathers came running forward to kill them both, but he was stopped by a beam of light.

Spirit Wolf spoke to Four Feathers, "You have not followed the laws of my ancestors!"

Spirit Wolf looked up at the sky and howled. As he howled, a beam of light from the sky came down and turned Four Feathers into dust! The people looked on in fear and was amazement at what happed to Four Feathers.

Spirit Wolf looked around at everyone and said, "Remember to follow the laws of your ancestors!"

Morning Star and Spirit Wolf walked away from the village. As they were walking away, Spirit Wolf turned back into a man.

Chapter Two

Shields

When you make a shield, mandala, medicine bag, or any other medicine item, your spirit enters what you created. Shields, like masks, have been important to people since the dawn of time. For any battle or combat situation, it is wise to seek protection. Shields have been a protective force in battle, be it physical, spiritual, emotional, or mental. Medicine shields are another form of the medicine wheel because they follow a circular pattern.

The difference between a shield and a mandala is, a mandala is hung on a wall in your home to bring you luck, protection, and happiness. A shield you carry, and it can be left outside your home to let people know where you live, who you are, and to protect you.

Besides protecting self, home or family, shields can be used to heal, to dream, and to show family clan, ledge, or social affiliation. Shields can be used to form an alliance with one's personal or tribal animal totem. Crest and shields tell stories or record important events.

Reasons for Making a Shield

Many stores sell shields and mandalas hanging on their walls. The general public buy shields or mandalas because they like the way they look, or perhaps the colors match a room in their home. They do not have the knowledge of the true meaning of a shield or mandala.

A friend once called me after she purchased a badger shield for her home. She didn't know why she and her husband were not getting along. When I walked into their home, I immediately noticed the badger shield on the wall. She said she bought the shield because it complemented the room. I told her to give the badger away to someone she didn't like. Once she got rid of the badger, everything returned back to normal. Badgers *hate* men.

Many female warriors would wear a badger into battle to give them the aggressive edge they needed. When you buy or make a shield, you should consider the characteristics of the animal you choose to bring into your home.

Many people possess more than one shield. One is a family shield, one is your public shield, and the other your personal shield. When I go to powwows and stay overnight, I hang my public shield on a pole outside my tent. It is about five inches wide. If I am with my family, I hang my family shield. A family pole is a large stick about six to eight feet you stick in the ground in front of your tent or camper. This pole represents all the members of your immediate family. There are many animal objects on the pole that represents my family clan and totems. When you make your family pole, you always leave a small branch sticking out to hang your shield on it.

How to Make a Physical Shield

The shield is a continuation of your personal medicine wheel. The animals, objects, and colors you pick represent your wheel. Because shield-making is complicated, you might prefer to get a shield from a good shield maker, store, or powwow vender. You can add the elements and feathers to it later. You can make your own shield with a hoop (embroidery), hide, metal, leather, cloth, or canvas.

Remember to smudge and center yourself first. Draw out your design on paper and wait at least one full moon before you paint your symbols. Remember this is not something you rush into; this is your medicine. This is the first thing people will see before they get to know you. When you are done, pray and ask the Great Spirit if the shield is good. If the answer is yes, then smudge the shield and give an offering in its honor. Sometimes you can design your shield in a day, some people take longer.

If you can think of something else, form a circle, and ft feels right to use it. Your spirit guide will not let you do something would be disrespectful to the Great Spirit and yourself. Remember if the shield doesn't feel right, then either bury it or put it in the trash can. If it is not blessed yet, don't throw out the objects you put on the shield. I burn my old shields.

Now that you have a circle to work with, you then decide what animal, skin, or cloth you are going to attach to your medicine wheel shield. Try not to use artificial fabrics because you are not fake, you are a real living being and so is your shield. If you have to use synthetic materials, then please make sure it is at least half cotton or another natural fiber. Lay your material down on a flat surface then put your ring on top of it.

Use chalk or a pencil and draw a line about five inches from the ring to give you plenty of overlap. If you overlap too much, it will bunch up in the back. Then attach your material in the back with sinew or cotton thread. Again, try to sew natural fibers. Many people use nylon thread because it doesn't rot or easily break. If you must use nylon thread, then please get it with some cotton in it. Try to take your time sewing the materials together. When you start to sew, either bring in the direction you were born or start in the direction where you live.

Now your shield is ready for your personal touches. Get out your medicine wheel and the design you picked for your shield. Some people paint their designs with acrylic paint and some use natural dyes such as flowers, grass, berries. I realize I told you not to use synthetic paint, but sometimes you have no choice.

I suggest you pencil in your design on your surface so you can erase any errors. Remember in Native American Indian medicine, "only the Great Creator is perfect." We make mistakes, and this is why there is an eraser at the end of a pencil.

If you make a mistake when you are painting, leave it, your spirit guide wanted it there for you. Don't get upset; sit back, wait then try again later. Maybe you were not ready to paint your shield at that particular time. I know people would correct the mistake, that is okay too. Remember, it's *your* shield.

If you want to glue something on your shield, I suggest you use either hot glue or another type of glue. There are many glues out there on the market, but please stay away from any glue that dries fast because it leaves no room for error. Superglue, I would not use. Once it's on there, it cannot be removed without ripping the fabric. If you want to use a natural approach, then use sap (pine tree), honey, or maple syrup.

Remember to smudge and center yourself first. When you are done, pray and ask the Great Spirit if the shield is good. If the answer is yes, then smudge the shield and give an offering in its honor. Some people might say "I didn't get an answer!" or "I prayed and prayed and nothing happened!" Please do not be discouraged; use your gut feeling. If your head says it's true and your heart says it's true and finally your stomach says it's true, it's correct. If there is any doubt in your mind, then put the shield away overnight, or one week, but no longer than twenty-eight days (a lunar month). If the shield looks and feels right, then it is; if not, then do it again.

I finished a shield for myself and was not getting answers. I sat there disappointed, wondering what I did wrong. A friend came over and *loved* the shield I made. The Great Spirit sent my friend to tell me the shield was good. I was pleased and thanked the Great Spirit for sending my friend to tell me the shield was fine.

How to Make a Spirit Shield

Try to remember when you were making your physical shield. Remember how you tried to make parts of the shield, and you couldn't get it to look the way you wanted it to. Perhaps the colors were not right. You might have wanted special fabric, not cotton or deerskin. Did you have trouble attaching the feather or another object to the shield? What if you did your shield and everything went right for you? Either way, you are about to make a spectacular shield!

In your imagination, and your spirit shield can be made of *any materials you want.* Solid gold, silver, the stars, sun, the moon, anything is possible! Why? Because it's your spirit shield, and it comes from your imagination!

One Medicine Woman spirit shield is made totally of different-colored roses. My spirit shield has the Earth spinning in the East, toward the Sun, the ocean moving in the West and the Fire Bird in the North. It's all held together with braided sweetgrass, vines and tree branches. You cannot be wrong in the design of your shield because it's yours and yours alone.

This is my favorite part: you can give your spirit shield magic superpower qualities to protect you. Can you sit on your spirit shield and fly? Does it shoot lightning bolts at an enemy? Can it provide comfort and joy to you when you are sad? Can your spirit shield talk, sing, or warn you of danger? Your spirit shield can be all and more. You can snap your fingers, whistle, or give your spirit shield a name when you want it to appear to you.

One simple rule you need to remember: you have to take care of your spirit shield, polish it, repair it, and keep it in good condition. When you are not feeling well and you look for your spirit shield, you will notice it will be damaged. This is because you are ill, and when your repair the shield, you will get better.

Finally, the spirit shield is just that—a shield to protect you. Don't allow anyone tell you that you can't do anything you want with your shield; they are jealous they do not have one.

Step-by-Step Guide for Making a Spirit Shield

First: find a place to meditate and have your physical shield in front of you. Call on your spirit guide to help you. Then, pray to the Great Creator for help, wisdom, and guidance.

Second: in your mind, stand, sit, or lay down in a space only you can enter. This is your private space and only people and animals can enter there. Even if some egomaniac tells you they are powerful and strong physically and spiritually, they cannot enter your space without your permission.

Third: begin drawing your shield. Remember, there are no limitations, anything you want or desire in a spirit shield is yours.

Fourth: begin creating your spirit shield, make it yours. Place whatever it takes to help you in, on, or around it. You will not and cannot be judged by anyone about what your spirit shield is made of.

Fifth: if you don't like what you created, take it away. Poof! It's gone, this is your reality. Recreate your spirit shield or keep the first one, it's your choice. If you are not sure about the spirit shield, then wait until the next full moon and look at it again. A good rule to follow is this: after thirteen full moons, if you still like the shield, it's yours.

Sixth: what superpowers can your spirit shield possess to protect you from all the sinister spirit things in your life? What is good about this is the spirit shield can never fail you unless you think it can. Go. Play with your spirit shield, see what it is capable of.

Seventh: take care of your spirit shield because it is a part of you. By cleaning the spirit shield, you are cleaning your spiritual health. If you do not feel well emotionally, the body will follow by becoming ill. Your mind is a powerful tool to a healthy body, mind, and spirit. If you believe you will get sick or better, you will. Mind over matter.

Personal Story: How Can I Fix My Shield?

I was at a powwow with Kat Pelletier "Medicine Woman," a woman wanted to know if I was the medicine woman who could help her with a problem. I answered, "I don't know. What's the problem?"

She said she had purchased a shield and when she got home, it didn't feel right. I asked her what was on it and she told me. I suggested one or more items on her shield should be removed and replaced with something else. She didn't know which ones to remove and she wanted me to tell her. I said it was not my shield, and she has the knowledge to do it herself. She looked at me with a pathetic stare. Kat was sitting nearby quietly observing the whole situation and looked at me, and I nodded to her that it was okay to interject. She stood up and gave the woman a demonstration on how her hands had energy. Kat stood face-to-face with her putting her hands palms out facing the woman. She told the woman not to touch her hands but to put her hands up facing her and to let her know when she started to feel energy or something different. About five inches apart, the woman started to feel something. Her right hand started to tingle, and she could feel Kats energy coming from her hands.

I said to her I was going to teach her how she could identify the object that was giving her shield a problem. I instructed her to turn her back, I was going to put four objects on the chair and cover them. I put my set of keys, my sunglasses, a small turtle shell, and my cell phone on the table.

I instructed her, "Please turn around. Now put your right hand over the sweatshirt covering the objects and in a clockwise motion, move your hand around the sweatshirt and find my cell phone."

She was very unsure at first, then I said, "You can do this!" I suggested to first go in a circle around the sweatshirt then go back and find the phone.

She hesitated at first but with Kat's and everyone's encouragement, she continued. She came back to one spot moving her hand back and forth and said, "I think the cell phone is here."

She lifted up the sweatshirt, and to everyone's amazement, she found my phone! She was so excited! Everyone congratulated her, and I said, "Now you can go home and take the object(s) out that do not belong on her shield."

Even though she purchased the shield, she was going to make it her own.

Chapter Three

Medicine Bags

As we move through this chapter, try to clear your mind of any preconceptions you might have about a medicine bag.

The medicine bag has been around since people decided to live and work together as a tribe or family unit. Every man and woman carried their own personal medicine bag. In addition to this, the medicine person would carry the herbs and sacred objects for the tribe and family.

The medicine people had many roles in the tribe. They were the priests, doctors, psychiatrists, and even acted as peacemakers during disagreements. The medicine people had tremendous power, sometimes even greater than the chief.

Often, the medicine people had several helpers. It was considered a great honor and privilege to be an apprentice. One of the many jobs was to carry the medicine bags and make them for the tribe or family.

If the medicine person did not have enough helpers, they would hide their medicine bags in different locations so they would not have to carry them when they moved from summer to winter camp locations. This was particularly true in the Northeastern areas. For example, medicinal herbs and sacred plants were grown in Assonet, Massachusetts, at Profile Rock. When different tribes passed through the area, they would barter with the medicine people to replenish their supply of herbs and plants and, also, to get plants and herbs they could bring back to grow on their own.

I have yet to meet a true medicine person that does not carry a well-stocked large bag that can be carried on their shoulder. This bag holds personal medicine and medicine objects which no one is allowed to see or touch. As we discuss the medicine bag in this chapter, I want to emphasize you should forget any preconceptions you might have about what a medicine bag should be. A Native American medicine bag is not the same as other medicine bags you might be aware of. Most of what we have come in contact with or read about claiming to be Native American bags are not.

Reasons for Making a Medicine Bag

For the most part, books on the market do not demonstrate knowledge of true native beliefs. Instead, they represent other forms of religion such as Wicca and New Age and call it Native American. A medicine bag is not necessarily for everyone. Many people have lived their lives without one. They have a medicine cabinet in their bathrooms or go to local pharmacy chains. For the Native Americans of the past, it wasn't a fashion statement to wear a medicine bag but rather a necessity. The Algonquin Indians carried their medicines in a leather bag or basket that was lightweight to travel with.

You will find many reasons for making a medicine bag and most of them will be wrong. The only reason for making a bag would be for your own personal and family medicine. You make a medicine bag because you personally want to make one, not because someone tells you to or because you have read about one or like someone else's bag.

Before the medicine cabinet became fashionable in the bathroom of the modern home, many homes had a medicine box or chest. If you visit a historic site such as Plymouth Plantation in Massachusetts, you will see the early settlers had a wooden medicine chest in their homes that held the popular folk remedies to treat illness.

One autumn, I became very ill with pneumonia, and I couldn't understand why. I decided to take out my medicine bag, but I could not find it. After finding the bag, I was upset about the poor condition it was in. As I looked the bag over, I realized I had ignored my medicine bag, and I allowed illness to enter my body. I quickly repaired the bag and replaced the old herbs with fresh ones. I started to feel better. By repairing the bag, I had strengthened my body and spirit.

Many medicine people have more than one medicine bag; one for public use, one for personal use, and one for healing. The medicine women I know have a public bag, a personal bag, and a tribal bag. Your medicine bag is an extension of yourself, whether it be physical or spiritual. Because your medicine bag is an extension of yourself, you should give a great deal of thought before you decide to make one.

My teacher always walked around with her bag, no matter where she went. One day she was talking to me and she came out with a beautiful, old porcupine quill bag. She told me it was her grandmother's medicine bag. I was surprised when she let me look at the bag and hold it. She offered the bag to the four directions and then to herself. After she spent almost an hour in prayer, she told me to smudge myself, the firepit, and any wood that would be needed to make a large hot fire. I followed her instructions and soon had the fire burning vigorously.

My teacher came out and looked at the fire. She proceeded to place the beautiful quill bag on the fire and sang to it and watched it burn. I stood there in shock and was amazed at what she had done. She turned to me and said, "It is of no use to me or anyone anymore."

The bag was her grandmother's personal medicine, and no one was allowed to possess it. I asked her why she didn't give the bag to a museum or to someone who would appreciate it. She said the bag was not meant to be hung in a museum or to be touched by people who did not have the belief in the Native American Indian ways. She spoke to me about an aspect of the medicine bag she had not revealed before. It was at this point she handed me her public medicine bag.

Some people might compare the medicine bag to a voodoo mojo bag because it uses pieces of your own hair or nails. Without divulging specific religious aspects of both the medicine and the mojo bag, it is sufficient to say anyone with the knowledge of how to use the bag could help or hurt you.

How to Make a Physical Medicine Bag

Before you begin to physically make your medicine bag, first visualize it in your mind. Once you have done this, you are ready to go on to the next step. What you think you want for a medicine bag may not be what you end up with.

Now you are ready to decide what materials you should use to make your medicine bag. You might choose to use leather, fur, wood, or cloth. There are many books on the subject of leatherwork. If you are not comfortable making your own bag using animal skins, then use vegan leather. You can also have someone make it for you or buy one. If you decide to buy a bag, you can make it your own by adding your own personal medicine items.

When I put coyote on my medicine bag I was aware of both the negative and positive sides of the animal. I had to recognize the coyote would tempt me to play practical jokes on people. I had to balance the coyote medicine with bear, which is why I have a pipestone bear on my bag. The one problem about the bear is bear has a tendency to attack first and ask questions later. The silver cones I put on the bottom of the bag act as a calming effect on the bear's aggressive nature. When the cones touch each other and make a bell-like sound, it frightens away the negative aspects of the coyote and bear.

Here are a few simple suggestions to make a basic medicine bag and you can try other techniques as well. If you want to make a small-sized bag, a large otter tail makes an excellent bag. It is flat and tapers to a point. All you have to do is fold the tail in three and sew up the two sides. The pointed end of the tail flaps over the top. You can sew on a braided strap and add your feathers, beads, shells, what have you.

You can make a simple bag out of a plain rectangle shape, either leather or both. Fold the material in three with the top falling half-way down over the bottom. Sew up each side and add a strap. It helps to support the top flap by sewing in a stick.

When picking animal parts, skin, or fur for your medicine bag, remember, you are using both the negative and positive aspects of the animal you have selected. This is why many people do not use animal parts but cloth or a wooden box. I don't blame them.

One of the medicine women's apprentices, named Winona, thought she could outsmart the animal spirits by picking "calm" animals for her medicine bag. First, she made the bag out of deerskin, then she added rabbit fur and a squirrel skull, thinking they were "harmless" animals. When she showed me her bag and told me she had pick all "gentle" animals, I looked at her and laughed! After a few weeks went by, Winona started to change, but not for the better. She began to hoard food, and if you touched her in any way, she would snap at you. If she became upset, she would shake uncontrollably.

One day when I was visiting the medicine woman, Winona's dearest friend, May "Little Star," asked Winona what she wanted to drink. Winona snapped back at Mary in such an uncharacteristic way that Mary yelled, "What the hell is wrong with you!"

I got up from my chair with my hands on my hips and said, "Have you looked at her medicine bag?" All the other medicine women were laughing because they knew what Winona's bag was made out of. Mary looked at the medicine women laughing, she looked at me laughing and said, "This can't be good. Winona, please let me see your bag." As she looked at the bag, Mary realized she had neglected her student and felt foolish for letting this happen.

She immediately removed the rabbit fur and squirrel skull from the bag, and Winona looked shocked and puzzled. She whined, "Aren't rabbits and squirrels gentle?"

Mary answered, "Yes, but what is the opposite of gentle?"

Winona sat down and thought about it. "How are the animals aggressive?" she asked.

Mary said, "Think about it."

Rabbits have a tendency to not like being touched, and they shake when they get upset. Squirrels hoard food for the winter. As Mary was telling Winona about this, Winona realized that she had to look at all the aspects of an animal before choosing one. She ended up using the deer and added the skunk and a bird to her bag. I go for what I like, full speed ahead.

The reason Winona picked the skunk is because it is gentle animal other animals stay away from because of the smell. She liked the idea it doesn't use physical violence to defend itself, but rather musky spray most animals find to be extremely offensive odor. She picked the bird because it is very hearty bird that does not migrate for the winter. It has keen survival skills, which Winona found useful. She was more likeable after she made these changes to her bag. The medicine women wanted me to emphasize thinking seriously selected items for your medicine bag. Give what you choose careful thought, don't pick something because it looks pretty or cute. Last, try not to overthink what your bag is going to be. You can drive yourself crazy doing that.

Always remember an animal has both a good side and a bad side which can be given to you without your knowledge. Don't be afraid to change anything you put on your bag. If it doesn't feel right to you, take it off the medicine bag.

How to Make a Spirit Medicine Bag

As you did with your physical medicine wheel, visualize in your mind what you would like your spirit medicine bag to look like. You must fully believe in whatever you imagine when making your spirit bag. You will return to your childlike beliefs that anything is possible before the adult world corrupted your mind. Think about Santa Claus and his magic bag that held an unlimited number of toys for all the children of the world. Remember you can use your imagination without any limitations because this bag exists only in your mind. It can be any size or shape, from the size of the palm of your hand to as large as you can carry. This bag is magical and is capable of holding anything you need, from magical weapons to the moon itself.

To make your spirit medicine bag, first, get yourself into a meditative state. Think about the kind of bag you want; what size, shape, materials, and colors. Think about the outside of the bag, the items inside the bag will come later. It takes time to visualize these things, so be patient. Remember that spirit medicine doesn't come overnight. Do not confuse the spirit medicine bag with creative visualization. Creative visualization works on the physical level to bring about physical manifestation. The spirit bag works on the spiritual level and does not involve any physical restraints. There are exceptions to most rules. In this case, medicine people can see spiritual things on the physical level. A medicine person is able to use a spiritual item on the physical level. Medicine people have a special ability to bring physical objects into the spiritual world, or to bring a spiritual object into the physical world. Medicine people can see a spiritual object in the physical world and identify it; or see a physical object in the spiritual world.

In my bag, I keep my white regalia that can never get dirty. It holds a knife that talks to me and warns me of any spiritual enemy. Another thing the bag holds is a double rainbow I take out if I need cheering up. The other things in my bag are too personal to mention. You can add or subtract items from your bag.

Once you are finished with your meditative state, you have to put everything back in your bag or it will disappear. You cannot leave the spirit world cluttered. There is a warning you should know about the items in your spirit bag. If you are in a meditative state and something or someone interrupts you, the items you have out of the bag will disappear. If you lose a simple item, you can get it back. If the item has been personalized for your use, such as my white regalia, then go back in the spirit world to find it by the next full moon. Don't worry if you cannot find what you lost, it will come back to you at the right time.

Guidelines for a Medicine Bag

1. Don't be afraid to change anything you put on or in your bag.
2. If the object you put on your bag doesn't feel right, take it off.
3. What you put in your medicine bag is no one's business but your own. If you wish to share this information with someone, please be careful.
4. When buying a medicine bag, do not let the salesperson know it is for you unless it will be your public medicine bag.
5. If you have someone make your bag, it must be someone you can trust.
6. When using your own hair, nails, or blood, on your personal medicine bag, remember to store the medicine bag in a safe place. This bag can be used against you for good or evil.
7. Remember to smudge yourself and all items you will use and put in your medicine bag.

Personal Story: Many Names Spirit Bag

The second time I met my teacher, she asked me to get an apple in the kitchen and bring it back outside to her. When I walked into the kitchen, my peripheral vision caught sight of a beautiful bag hanging on the wall. I picked up the apple, turned around, and there was nothing on the wall. I knew I was not imagining things, so I closed my eyes and when I opened them again, the bag was there.

Without taking my eyes off the bag, I became attracted to the bluish-black fur on the bag and was compelled to walk over to it and touch it. As I touched the bag, a strange feeling rushed through my body. I walked outside and handed the apple to my teacher. I told her

I had felt the fur on the bag hanging in the kitchen and wanted to know what it was. My teacher bolted over to me and slapped my face hard enough to make it sting. I was being reprimanded for touching her bag.

My teacher's apprentice was sitting there and asked, "What bag? I never saw a bag on the wall."

My teacher put her hands on my shoulders and then moved one hand to my head. She grabbed my wrist and said, "Let's go in the house."

Her apprentice said, "Show me this bag that you see," in an arrogant tone. I pointed to the bag, and the apprentice said, "I don't see it."

I looked at my teacher; I did not know what to do. I watched as the apprentice put her right hand through the bag and banged on the wall. The bag was invisible to her. My teacher told her apprentice to go outside and get an armful of firewood, and she walked out haughtily. My teacher then put her right hand on my shoulder and asked me to describe the bag. After I described the bag, my teacher put both her hands on my shoulders and said, "The spirits have sent you to me."

I asked if I could touch the bag again, and she looked at me sternly and said, "*No*!"

Then, with a catlike grin, she said, "That's my spirit bag. This knowledge is not to be freely given to anyone."

Chapter Four

Balancing Your Wheel

Time and Patience

I am asking two things of you before you read this chapter: time and patience. First, get a desk lamp or a strong light. Next get a white piece of paper. Place your hand about eight inches from the light and in between place the paper so you can see the outline of your hand. Look at your shadow of your hand; it should be fuzzy around the edges. Move your open hand slowly closer to the paper. Notice something about your shadow? The shadow of your fingers on the paper are becoming sharp and more defined. Good. That is the idea behind holding your hand over the object in your wheel.

Many people have a wonderful gift of knowing instantly if a medicine wheel feels right. Me? It took years of training and experience to get it right. It did not come easy to me. When you look at a medicine wheel and it "looks" too perfect, it is because it is not. Looks can be deceiving.

Please imagine a nice new vehicle. Brand-new, no rust, chrome, tires shiny, everything on the outside is great. Inside, the seats are nice and clean, the dash neat, the steering wheel has a new leather cover on it. The engine is in top condition. You get the idea.

You sit in the vehicle, put the key in the ignition, and the vehicle will not start. You cannot adjust the mirrors or the seat. The radio and horn do not work. But the vehicle looks good! Why doesn't the vehicle work? Answer: no battery or gas. Isn't that interesting.

Without the battery and gas, the vehicle would not work or move. Same goes for the medicine wheel. It can look nice and perfect, but it doesn't work. You are missing the spirituality and the energy flow.

I said in the past, you can make your medicine wheel from almost anything. Remember this, remember this well: "Any man-made synthetic object does not hold energy. Plastic, polyester, anything not natural will never—yes, I said *never*—holds energy." It has to be a basic elemental relation, rock, tree, water, one of our relations. The energy and spirituality will not recognize the hosts.

Do you own your own vehicle? Have you ever let anymore borrow it or had it serviced? The second you sit in the driver's seat, you know it is not right for you. They always move the seat forward, back, closer, further back, up or down. They change the steering wheel height, but worse, they play with your mirrors. You have to readjust all this to your height and size. Same with the medicine wheel.

Another example: I dislike buying new clothes pick off the rack. Worse, you have to go into a dressing room to take off your clothes to try on the new ones. Once you have on the new clothes, you look in the mirror to see how you look. You either like the way you look or not. Either the clothes will feel right, or you do not feel comfortable. Same with the medicine wheel.

Head, Shoulders, Knees, and Toes—Can You Feel It?

When setting up your medicine wheel, first put the wheel together the way you think it should go. Walk around the medicine wheel clockwise (unless your below the equator then its counter clockwise) starting at the direction you are comfortable with. You do the main four directions first. I clap and rub my hands together to get the energy going. You stand next to the direction, place your hand or hands over the rock or object then you will know if it feels right. You walk around the wheel with your hand extended over the rocks. When I am done, I shake my hands away from my body and the medicine wheel.

The energy you will feel in your hands is different for everyone or the same. I feel heat and tingling. My friend feels a cold sensation coming from her fingers up her arms. My other friend feels numbness in his hands, feet, and toes. I thought, *Your feet?* Sometimes I might even get light-headed or dizzy from the energy that is not correct. I suggest when you are in bed at night, rub your hands or clap them together hard. When you do this, hold your hands in a prayer fashion, palms facing each other apart about one inch or more. You will feel energy as if you have an invisible cotton ball between your hands. You will be able to bounce your hands back and forth. You don't have to do this at night, you can try it in the daytime. Whatever works for you.

If you do not have this ability, you can use a smudge stick or sage. Hold the sage or smudge stick next to the area in questioned. If the smoke rises in a straight line or swirling, the placement is correct. If the smoke goes everywhere but on your spot, remove the object and put something else in its place. I realize this is tedious, but if you want the medicine wheel to work properly it will take time and patience. Once all the rocks or objects are in place, you walk around the medicine wheel several times to make sure it is balanced. When your wheel is balanced, oh, what a feeling of joy! I compare this to walking up to an electric eye door and the door magically opens up.

Mister Sir Anthony "Broken Eagle Claw" said, *"When you get a new tire for your vehicle, they balance and align it. You have a tire by itself, it's perfect, but when you put it on a rim, it becomes part of an assembly, and now the parts must be balanced together."* Same for the medicine wheel.

I have been to many outside medicine wheels, and I immediately know if it is balanced or not. The first clue would be if the wheel looks too perfect. Many people put one color stone on the outside and another color on the inside. Putting quartz stones does not guarantee a medicine wheel will produce energy and spirituality. I have seen the funniest, odd-shaped stones in medicine wheels and the energy was phenomenal! Please do not fall into the thought where you are determined to put a stone from one area in the direction it came from. It might not like it there. What you want is not what the medicine wheel wants. I helped a friend build a wheel, and they wanted the stone that came from one of the Great Lakes in the north, but the wheel did not feel balanced. He changed all the stones around it but still, it didn't work. When he moved the stone in the west direction, *voila*, the wheel went crazy, spinning, my ears ringing from the wheel being so pleased.

Kat Pelletier, Medicine Woman, was with a medicine group from a local college visiting a museum in New Hampshire. Kat thought she did not have the ability to know if a medicine wheel had energy or not. Her spirit guide had something else in mind. When she was walking the wooded pathway, she came upon a medicine wheel. It was the same dark colored stone on the outside ring and milky quartz stone in the inner circle. She knew immediately that it had no energy, there was nothing. A woman from the group came behind Kat, they both agreed the wheel had no energy. After discussing the wheel, they both agreed the wheel should be rebuilt in another location with other stones.

When visiting Kat, our friends who live on the Vermont-New York border call Kat to come see their new medicine wheel she and her husband made in their backyard. I was excited because I knew they both had Native American Indian heritage and knowledge. We sat down in their living room drinking coffee, and she started talking about their medicine wheel and what they put in it. My heart sank as she described the special, loved objects put in the wheel. I looked at Kat, and we both smiled. We got up and went to the backyard to see their special powerful wheel. The medicine wheel looked pretty and whimsical with plastic unicorns, stars, angels, and other mythical animals. They were so proud and happy with their wheel constantly saying, "Can you feel the power?" I nodded my head with my hands in my pockets and didn't say a word. I was not going to burst their bubble, telling them the medicine wheel had no energy or spirit in it. They were happy with what they did, and I let it go. Sometimes you have to balance your friendship over what you know is wrong. Yes, Kat and I could have told them their medicine wheel was terrible but we both agreed they would not have listened to us. Kat did try later to tell and show them, but they wanted nothing to do with it.

They said it was already pretty, it wasn't dealing with what the spirits wanted but the way it looked. Sometimes you have to make a judgement to keep your mouth shut.

Still not sure what to do? Don't worry, I hope what I am about to say will help you. No one or medicine wheel is perfect. You are not perfect. Your medicine wheel will not be perfect. Why? Only God, the Creator, is perfect. You and the medicine wheel are always changing.

You could set up your wheel one week or month, then go back; the medicine wheel will not feel right to you. Change it. That is the fun and enjoyment of the medicine wheel. It is a living, energy, constantly changing, just like you.

I will admit my four direction animals, trees, and rock have not changed in years. But the animals that surround them I changed constantly. I made my wheel from a skipping stone kit, gluing pictures of different animals, stones, and trees on each one. I sometimes put the main directions and leave the rest with blank skipping stones. The reason I use skipping stones is I can place a claw from an animal, a stone, or a piece of bark on top of them. Works for me.

If you still do not understand energy and spirit, I suggest you find a medicine person or someone who understands metaphysical energies and speak with them. If you do find someone, and you are still at a lost, you are blocking yourself from the knowledge and experience. You need to relax, stop judging yourself and thinking you are a failure. If at first you don't succeed, try, try again. Failure to me translates to experience. Rethink your thoughts for good and not bad.

People can be their own worst enemy. When someone asks me to help them and I hear the phrase "I can't," I tell them to come back when they remove the word "can't" from their vocabulary. Sometimes I feel they are wasting my time, but it's not my decision, so I question them further.

"How many times have you meditated? How many times have you sat quietly, alone, just being one with your surroundings and the Creator? Did you do any of the tasks?"

If they answer "A few times," I tell them to come back when they have done these task the amount twice their age. You should see the look at their faces. Shock, disbelief, and anger. What I ask you to do, I have done myself. Try not to be so hard on yourself. The Chinese have a game (a small paper tube) you put your pointed fingers in it. The more you resist and pull, the tighter it becomes. When you relax your two fingers, the game releases its hold on you and you are free. Once you remove doubt in your mind and you put in "I can do this," everything will change. Success! Be kind to yourself.

I always joke, "What is the difference between a medicine person and a shaman? A thousand dollars." Shaman training costs more than becoming a medicine person. The name "Shaman" is not indigenous to Turtle Island, but it came from the Tuntus People in Siberia. I know a person who has many certificates saying she has gone through these shamanic trainings. Some were one-day seminars, others a weekend. Know, you do not pay to become a medicine person or shaman or as I like to say, "shawoman." Only the Great Creator can pick who is going to be a medicine person or shaman. My family has a tradition of medicine people, and sometimes it skips a generation. You do not pick spirit; spirit picks you, dragging, kicking, and screaming you go.

Please do not let anyone tell you, you cannot do it. The fact is, if spirit did not want you to do it, then you would not have known about the medicine wheel. You were meant to do this, follow your dreams, your bliss. Better to have failed trying then not having tried at all. Regret is a terrible thing. I am confident you will succeed. You are special and I hope we meet in the future. Aquene.

By Golly, I Think I Got It!

Isn't it a wonderful feeling you can actually feel the energy of your medicine wheel. Every time you sit down at your wheel, you scan your hand over your wheel and spin it. Nice. You have friends come over and ask about your medicine wheel. You show them and they stand there looking at you as if you are crazy, or they, too, feel the energy of the wheel. Some friends might even say, "Show me how you did this, I love it!" Show them; share your wonderful experience with them. To the ones who feel nothing, help them if they want. If they cannot get it, do not worry. It's not your problem; it's theirs.

I appreciate the joy and moment when someone finally experience the energy from their wheel. The look on their faces is pure joy! One person said to me they thought they would never feel the energy of the wheel but when it did happen, *Pow! Zing! Bang!* (Sorry, I watched too much *Batman* when I was young!) Some people say they can see the energy of the wheel. One person described it as the Sun hitting the pavement, seeing the heat waves as it comes off the road.

A guest came to my home; they looked at my medicine wheel, said to me, "Your wheel is out of balance."

What? No. I walked over to my wheel and it was. I lit my sage, looked at my wheel, and noticed a piece was missing. It fell on the floor. Whew! When I put it back, all was good again. Please remember, no one is perfect; only the Great Spirit, Creator, God.

I was invited to a place in Attleboro, Massachusetts, to make a medicine wheel. The people are wonderful and spiritual there. Good energies. There were a few New Age people there, bragging how many classes and certificates they had to the guests. Everyone was wondering who was going to make the wheel and when. I stood there observing, listening to everyone talking, laughing, and judging. Finally, the couple who owns the property came forward to introduce me. The room stopped being friendly and all eyes were on me. The Great Creator does have a sense of humor; the second they said I was a Native American Indian, all smiles went up in the room. They wanted to know where I got my training and certificates. They didn't ask who trained me, who was my medicine teacher or what experiences I had making the wheel. I said, "I have no certificates because you do not pay for spirituality."

They did not like my answer; it went over like a lead balloon. I shared how and who trained me, they all looked at each other, and some even laughed a little.

I stepped back and asked, "Who has the sage pot to light?" Once everyone was smudged, we went outside to make the wheel. Their certificates did not teach them about the energies in their hands and body. Once everyone understood what I was doing, things went right along. It was a good day and experience, and I made some new friends. I hope you will be able to share your experiences with old and new friends. *Aquene.*

Eileen Builds a Medicine Wheel on the Beach

I felt the earth beneath my feet, the wind on my face, and the waves gently surrounding my feet and ankles as the water bent the reflection of the Sun's ray.

I made small medicine wheels in the house on the table or the floor, but I never made a large wheel outdoors for myself. The largest wheel I ever made was approximately eleven feet in diameter. I wanted to create a large medicine wheel and thought the beach would be great! After thinking about several locations, I decided on Gooseberry Island in Westport, Massachusetts. On the beach, my intention was to build a large medicine wheel of over thirty-three feet in diameter. I wanted to have the experience of building a large medicine wheel outdoors.

First, I smudged the area, then measured the location. I rolled four boulders a little smaller than a basketball to mark the four directions and one rock for the Great Creator.

The second day I smudged the area again then concentrated on building the outer circle with rocks. The circle was set up along the edge of water where I hoped the high tide would cover the wheel. As I sat there, the tide was coming in and got very excited when I realized the wheel was going to be completely covered by water.

I walked around the medicine wheel circle to see if any rock was out of place. I thought it looked fine. I stood with my hands on my hips, I thought to myself the wheel doesn't feel right. I could not feel the energy flow.

I stood in the east direction, closed my eyes, and put my hand over the rocks. The wheel did not feel balanced. I walked around the medicine wheel slowly to find several rocks out of balance. Once I switched or removed the rocks, I could feel the swirling energy of the medicine wheel circle. Now the wheel was complete. I gave thanks to the Great Creator and left offerings of bread and corn for the animals.

One afternoon, I visited the medicine wheel. It was completely underwater! When I saw the medicine wheel underwater, it appeared to be in another world. I quickly lit my sage bowl and walked into the wheel to experience the energy flow. Suddenly, all the elements hit me at once: earth, air, water, fire, and spirit!

First, I felt the earth beneath my feet then the wind on my face. The waves were gently surrounding my feet and ankles as the water bent the reflection of the Sun's ray that came shining down. As I looked up at the sky, I heard thunder and saw lightning in the distance.

I guess that represents fire, I thought to myself. *I better get out of the water before the lightning has me experience spirit.*

I sat on the beach, enjoying the medicine wheel under water, such a beautiful sight. As I walked back to my car, it started to rain, hard. On the way home, I felt more centered and one with the earth than I did earlier that day. All I kept thinking was, *What would a bigger medicine wheel feel like?*

Yep.

My friends who run the Medicine River Powwow in Gilbertville, Massachusetts, have a permanent powwow circle in their backyard. Every winter, the river overtakes the land and covers the powwow circle with three to four feet of water. The water cleanses the powwow wheel and gives back good energy and spirit to the wheel.

Chapter Five

Native American Indian Music

Music is an essential and important key to the medicine wheel. If you are hearing impaired, you can feel the pulse of the music in the vibration of the drum. Music makes an important contribution to spiritual rituals and the awakening of your spirituality.

This is the reason I decided to include music in the advanced guide. All creatures respond to the sound and vibration of music. Animal and even plants are known to respond to music. Music is one of the oldest forms of communication known to man.

Indians have a subconscious sense of harmony. Indian music has three basic purposes: ceremonial, religious, and entertainment. Although much of the music could be called entertainment, the ceremonial and religious aspects can be hidden in the music to those who do not know.

To give an example of three types of music, I will talk about the modern powwow (gathering). The opening and closing of the powwow are ceremonies (traditions). The religious part of the powwow is the smoking of the pipe privately before the powwow begins. The dance competitions are the entertainment part of the powwow. Please do not confuse the nondance competitions, such as the Crow Hop, the Grass Dance, the Snake Dance, for example.

The first characteristic of Indian music is the declining trend of the melodic line. The melody usually starts on a high note and ends on a low note. Indian music of the part used five basic tones.

They usually start out on the F note and end around the D note. Indian music is also nonharmonic music. It is difficult to keep up a harmony. Indians sing the rhythm of a song the way it was taught to them. They do not use written music and people often say they have a scale of their own.

The second characteristic of Indian music is the timing changes from one measure to the next. The flute might be playing one rhythm and the drum another at the beginning of the melody, but they will end up with the same rhythm in the end.

A third characteristic of Indian music is it possesses more rhythm than harmony. The rhythm of a love song is much slower than the rhythm of a war chant. The beat of the Indian drum possesses a hypnotic quality. The rhythms of the various instruments possess magical characteristics. When a man or woman plays a love song on the flute for a man or a woman, it is very hard for them to resist the hypnotic sound.

Chanting

Why do natives sing? Because they are calling on the spirits. Chanting and singing was and is a way to elevate human power to raise his or her voice in prayer.

With early Native American music, you have to keep in mind that the prehistoric indigenous people of the Americas did not have a formal oral or written language. They used pictures, sign language, facial expressions, and guttural sounds of communicating. However, they always had music.

When I was young, I met an old Indian man in his late nineties who never spoke. He only communicated by using sign language, laughter, and tears for his entire life.

One night, to my surprise, he got up and started beating the drum. He sang slowly, using only syllables in the most beautiful voice I have ever heard.

"Hey ya ho, hey ya, ha, hey ya hey, ya, ha, hi ya, hey ya hey ya ha hi ya." He sang the basic syllables of primitive Indian chanting that had been passed down for generations.

When you listen to music, you know immediately whether you are listening to a sad song or a happy song by the tempo, tone, and movement of the music. Many native songs are done in a minor key because they are meant to sound spiritual. If you don't agree with this, try singing "Jingle Bells" in a minor key at a slower tempo. Using a minor key gives a serious and sad quality to the music. Always keep in mind the main purpose of Indian music was to benefit the individual or tribe.

Music was used in ceremonies to bring rain, to produce good crops, and to call on the animal spirits for a good hunt, etc. Music was also used by medicine people for healing individuals. Modern-day Indians still use music for the benefit of all rather than for the approval of an audience. A man might desire to excel in singing because he wants to lead the group of singers or drummers. Modern customs have brought new songs to the Native American by composing and adapting Indian melodies for band instruments. However, the old songs about mystery and power are held close to the heart of the few who love them and still follow the old ways.

Drumming

Of all the drumming groups I have heard, the most original and true sound is Soaring Eagle Singers under the direction of Chief Don Sly of the Aquidneck Indian Council, Portsmouth, Rhode Island.

In Native American drumming, each beat has a special meaning. The natives use the drum to communicate with people just as the church bells were used in colonial times. In modern times, the church bells rang at the end of World War II. I remember the church bells ringing the day President Kennedy was shot in Dallas, Texas, on November 22, 1963. It's a powerful communication tool.

When at powwow, as I approach the circle, I know what dance or event is going on by the beat of the drum. All drumbeats are based on 4/4 time (1-2-3-4).

There are many different kinds of drumbeats, and each tribe uses their own special drumbeats, depending on the drummers. Here are a few examples:

The *spiritual drumbeat* is you talking to the Creator alone. It is the same as the prayer drumbeat at powwows. The rhythm is: *beat (count) 2-3-4*. You do not hit the drum on the numbers. You do not dance to this.

The *group prayer* rhythm is this: *beat-beat, 3-4*.

To *call people to council*. The rhythm is this: *beat-beat-beat-4*.

The *war beat* that we call the Hollywood movie beat. The rhythm is this: *hard beat, soft-soft-soft* with the heavy accents on the first beat of the drum. Many drummers will not play this beat.

The *healing drumbeat* uses the rhythm: *hard-soft-3-4*. This is also called the *heartbeat* rhythm.

The *storytelling beat* uses the rhythm: *hard-hard-soft-4*.

The *bad-news beat* is hard soft and is played continuously.

The drumbeats I have described are basic, traditional drumming techniques. At some point of each song, chant or dance, you will usually hear the drums beat hard. People who are dancing will raise their arms in the air.

The part of the drum you hit also affects the loudness of the beat as well as the pitch. Many tribal drummers will follow dancers. This is especially true if the dancers performs in front of the drummers. A drummer can make or break a dancer.

The loud (strong heartbeat) drumbeat is hit in the center of the drum which represents the Great Creator. The soft drumbeat is hit on the outer edge of the drum that represents you and the drummers. When a group of people get together to drum they can begin by doing a hard-soft drumbeat slowly to call everyone together. After everyone has joined in and drumming together, the heartbeat rhythm gets the drummers working together.

Many of the Northeastern Indians did not have drums. When the British and French came to the East Coast, they introduced drums to the Algonquin Indians.

The Southwestern and Midwestern Indians use large round drums similar to the base drum. The tom-tom is played by one person, but the large, round tribal drum can be played by several people at once.

The Northwestern Indians use individual round drums which range from one to three inches in width. The Northwestern round drums are open in the back where they are laced together with a handle. The tom-tom and large round tribal drums are closed on the bottom.

I am not going to get into who can play on a drum. Many will say only men can drum, many like a mix drum (male-female). I am not getting into that argument. I have been to many functions and gatherings where friends become enemies.

Most drums are round because they represent the circle of life. The octagonal (eight-sided) drum represent all the directions. East, southeast, South, southwest, West, northwest, North, and Northeast.

Many people decorate their drums by painting designs on them to know where to hit the drum. The design on your drum might indicate your clan or totem animal. Remember, you are calling on the spirit of whatever you paint on your drum.

If you are thinking of making your own drum, I suggest you don't if you value your sanity. Think of what might go wrong and it will. If you insist on punishing yourself needlessly, get a drum kit. If someone tells you it is easy to make a drum, then ask them to show you how to do it. If they are willing to show you, then pay attention, take pictures, and learn. You might have beginner's luck, but if not, buy one. You might even find a design painted on a drum which appeals to you if you are not artistically inclined. My family are drum makers, and I have made many different drums.

Rattles

Most tribes of Indians have some form of rattle. Rattles were used for shamanic rituals and ceremonies. The medicine people used rattles to treat the sick by scaring away their illness. There are three basic types of rattles. The first type of rattle uses some kind of container (such as a horn, a shell, or a gourd) that is filled with something like pebbles, beans, corn, or anything small that could move around in the rattle to make a noise.

The second type of rattle has some type of handle (usually made of wood or bone) with objects attached to the end (deer toes, bells, metal cones, shells, teeth, dew claws) which makes noise. This rattle is used for blessing and for communicating with the spirits. Some tribes attach bells or deer toes around their ankles for dancing and ceremonies.

The third type of rattle is a ratchet-style percussive instrument. It is made by notching a stick and using another stick or bone to rub against the notched stick. Two bones were frequently used for this type of rattle. In the mid-western tribes, they used the notched buffalo rib bone and even a horse's jaw bone with the teeth as a ratchet with another stick or bone. The Micmaq Indians would use an ash tree branch and split it to make their rattles.

The South American Indians had a tube-shaped rattle about six feet long and six inches wide and was made from a cactus. First, they would dry out a cactus and push the needles inside. Then they would fill the cactus with tiny pebbles. They would seal off each end with either a piece of wood or leather. They would use this rattle to bring rain, and it was called a "rain stick."

You do not have to worry about whether or not a rattle will work in the damp air because it will. You cannot bang a drum made of rawhide skin when it is wet. I enjoy a rattle; when I get one in my hands, I do not stop making plenty of noise.

Flutes

Flutes are as old as the world. Flutes vary in material they are made of, depending on the natural environment of the area. They could be made of wood, bone, bamboo, gourds, clay. The wide variety of materials only needed to be able to have holes made in them to be made a flute.

Flutes have three purposes in the tribe. First, they are used by the medicine people for healing; second, they are used for entertainment; and third, they are used by young people to court their mate (and hopefully hit all the right notes).

To show how important flute playing is to the Southwest Indians, the legends of Kokopelli, the humped back flute player, go back ten thousand years or more. His likeness is found on petroglyphs from thousands of years ago.

Kokopelli went to one of the sky spirits to get seeds for his people. He played his magical flute, which put the sky spirit to sleep. He then stole the seeds and carried them off on his back. He brought corn, beans, squash, tobacco, and flowers back to his people. When the sky spirit woke up and realized his seeds had been stolen, he told the Great Creator. The Great Creator punished Kokopelli giving him a hump on his back from that day on.

When people first hear flute music they immediately become quiet. Some people say the flute music sounds magical, calming, and seductive. Many flute players call the hymn “Amazing Grace” a Cherokee hymn, but it is not. It is a Christian antislavery hymn written by Englishman John Newton.

Personal Story: We Heard You Drumming

I had decided to visit to my friend’s home near Kearsarge Mountain in New Hampshire for a short vacation. I brought my drums and rattles along to play by an open firepit. All the way up, I was excited about drumming with my friends.

That day we dug the firepit, looked for rocks and wood. Everyone was all excited by the thought of the drumming we were going to do that evening. One person couldn't stay because she was responsible for the cabins on Lake Winnipesaukee. She left thinking about us all the way home.

We had supper, cleaned up, and walked down to the firepit. The drums were a little warped by the weather so we placed them near the fire to warm up. My friend led the welcoming ceremony, and we all sat down to drum.

Medicine Hawk was to my right. He is a stone and woodcarver; he does excellent work. He sometimes thinks men are better than women, but we always remind him women are more superior. There were two males and four females not counting the dogs and part wolf.

It was a beautiful full moon that night. We started with the drum heart beat for a personal healing. It surrounded us just like the moonlight, *boom, boom, boom, boom, boom.*

We drummed nonstop for twenty-five minutes. The sound of our drumbeats danced across the sky for everyone to hear. All of a sudden, Medicine Hawk's drumstick head flew off his stick, and we all laughed.

We all yelled, "A-HO!"

Our bodies, mind, spirit, and our surroundings were buzzing with energy; it was a natural high for us all.

We went to sleep that night still feeling the good natural high from the drumming. The next day we got a call from people who were staying at the cabins at Lake Winnipeasukee. They were lying in bed, looking at the moonlight shining through their windows when they heard and felt the energy from the drums.

We were astonished but not surprised. They said the drumming sounded as if we were on the lake in a boat. Everyone looked at each other. It was one of the best drumming experiences I ever had!

When I arrived home, there was a message on my answering machine. It was my friend's daughter who was staying on the opposite side of Lake Winnipeasukee. She also heard the drumming and knew it was me making all the noise. When I explained to her where we were drumming, she was amazed. She said it sounded like we were just across the lake.

I thought this had to be a coincidence, a hundred miles away they heard us drumming? Two days later, I received a telephone call from my friend and his wife, who live near the Vermont border, and they heard us drumming. They knew my style of drumming and could recognize it resonating through the air. I had to sit down on that one.

When I thought this drumming business was over, I received another telephone call, this time from my old friends in Massachusetts near the New Hampshire border. You guessed it, they heard us drumming! They were also outside admiring the full moon as they heard our drumming.

So next time you are sitting near the top of a mountain, make sure your drumming is of good intentions because you will never know who will be listening.

Amerindian Legend: Singing Bird and Whistling Wind Find Music

Many moons ago, there was ice and snow everywhere. There were woolly mammoths and saber-toothed tigers roaming the earth. The early Indian's main concern was survival. They needed to hunt for food, keep warm, and make clothing. They had no time for anything else. Men and women did not live long, and life was filled with hardships.

As the ice melted and the weather became warmer, people began to live longer. Where the land was once barren, trees and plant life now grew. The lakes were filled with fish and plant life for the people to eat. As time passed, the days grew longer and became easier to survive.

One day, a boy and girl were walking through the woods picking berries. The sweet music of the birds caught their attention. The boy wondered if he could make that sound and the girl encourage him to try. At first, he couldn't make the sounds of the birds, but as he kept on trying, he was successful.

"That sounds beautiful," said the girl.

"Can you sound like another bird?" she asked.

They continued on walking through the forest listening for songs from other birds. When they returned to their village they went to the elders to show them what they had learned. The elders were pleased and invited the children to come to the fire circle that night to show the others what they learned. From one moon to the next, the children went out to the woods to learn more birdsongs.

One day, as the boy was whistling and the girl singing, they stopped by last year's vegetable garden. There was a dried gourd lying on the ground. When the girl picked up the dried gourd she shook it. It made a tiny rattling sound.

"Listen to this!" she said to the boy excitedly. He stopped to listen to the girl rattling the gourd.

"What kind of sound would it make if we put rocks in it?" he asked.

They searched the ground for small pebbles to put in the gourd. What a sound it made!

"It is so loud, it sounds like a rockslide!" the girl shouted. They decided to call this a rattle because of the sound it made.

When they returned to the village, they showed the elders the rattle they made. The elders were pleased and invited the children to come to the fire circle that night to show the people. From one moon to the next, the children went out to the woods and learned many more ways to make different rattles.

One day as the children were walking through the marshlands, the girl snapped of a large reed and began to blow into it. The reed did not make any noise so she put the reed down and stepped on it by mistake. When she picked it up again there were holes in it. She tried to cover the holes with her fingers as she blew into the reed again, but she could not cover the hole nearest her mouth. She made a flute! She quickly learned she could make different sounds by moving her fingers in different positions.

When they returned to the village, they showed the elders the new reed they made. The elders gave it the name "flute." The elders were pleased and invited the children to come to the council fire that night to show the villagers how to make a flute.

At the fire circle, the elders were chanting, the men and women using the rattles—they were all happy. They decided it was time to give the boy and girl a name for what they had given to the people. They had shown wisdom and responsibility in what they had done. The girl would be called "Singing Bird," and the boy would be called "Whistling Wind."

Chapter Six

Sweat Lodge

Wherever you go in the world, you will find a culture that has something comparable to a sweat lodge. A sweat lodge is made specifically to make you sweat out impurities in your body and mind. A sweat lodge can be dry or wet heat, depending on the culture. Some cultures use both. Dry saunas do not use any water for steam. They create dry heat similar to a desert environment. The wet sauna uses water which is poured over the rocks to create wet steam.

The Scandinavians were the first ones to identify the skin as the "third kidney." They are still known throughout the world for their health spas. Many of the wet and dry redwood saunas found throughout the world were designed by Scandinavians. They believed by using the sauna you would stay healthy.

The Roman culture introduced hot baths wherever they conquered. These are similar to the wet saunas or sweat lodge because they were used for purification and relaxation. In the Roman culture, hot baths were not for the common man. They were used by people of wealth and power. Political meetings were informally held in the hot baths and many decisions were made there. Sadly, it was used for prostitution and sex with children and adults.

When the Romans went to Egypt, they found similar hot baths. The basic difference was the Egyptians used aromatic oils and herbs in the baths. The Egyptians used salt and sulfur baths for healing purposes. Many of the herbs used in the baths were similar to the native culture.

The natives used the sweat lodge for purification and spirituality, depending on the location and the tribe. People in general are more familiar with the Southwestern and Plains tribes' version of the sweat. The difference between the sweat lodges has a great deal to do with the geography of the land and the animals that are indigenous to the area. The Northeast does not have deserts and the West does not have our oceans or caves.

When you are invited or requested to do a sweat, make sure you know the people involved.

Many people offer a sweat lodge for money and this is wrong! You should not pay for spiritual medicine! Anyone who charges a fee for a sweat is deceitful. The sweat should be near a stream, river, pond, or ocean. Why? You need to cool your body down gently after you leave the sweat. This is also where they get the water to pour over the rocks in the sweat.

The sweat lodge is a place where you are about to talk with the Great Spirit. You should approach the Great Spirit with respect with your head facing Mother Earth and crawling on your hands and knees.

To prepare for your sweat, I suggest you fast. Practice your fasting three weeks ahead of time, then fast three days before. This means no alcohol, candy, meat, junk food or cigarettes. Eat nuts, fruit, vegetables, juice and water.

The next step is to stop swearing (if you do) and stop saying negative remarks. You don't want to be swearing and then speak to the Great Spirit with the same tongue. Try putting your mind in a positive state.

When you begin your first sweat, you should not stay in it for more than fifteen minutes consisting of three- to five-minute intervals. A person will lift the flap of the sweat and place new rocks in the firepit in the middle after every five minutes, then the flap will be lowered again. Do not use beach rocks because the water that is in them will cause them to explode.

Please do not get macho and feel you can stay in the sweat lodge longer than anyone else. It is not a contest; a sweat is not a game or meant for competition. It is not the same as your club sauna or your own personal steam bath. You are sitting on Mother Earth and are subject to her will.

You should be naked; however, if you are uncomfortable with that then wear a bathing suit. Please do not wear any jewelry, especially a watch.

When you feel ready, you can increase the time to about ten-minute intervals and up to twenty-minute intervals for no more than three total hours of time. People that do a long sweat have had many years of experience and knowledge of medicine.

Reasons for a Sweat

Sweat lodges are divided into two categories: male and female. Men and women should not share a sweat lodge. Men and women give off different odors, and the energies are different.

During the period of time your body is sweating, it is dehydrating. You should only replace the water you have lost with natural water. During a sweat, I suggest you keep your eyes closed. When you open them, your eyes will tear to allow the impurities to come out of your tear ducts. I find the herbs sting my eyes. It is easier to meditate with my eyes closed.

The sweat lodge consists of four elements: earth, air, fire, and water. When you have a problem, you would first sit in the corner of the direction in which your element is located. I do not mention spirit because you represent spirit and you call on the Great Spirit to be with you.

Technically, earth, air, fire, and water are not considered elements in modern science. The Greeks included these four as elements in their science because they believed them to be the four basic qualities that made up all substances.

The Pesuponcku: the Men's Sweat

The first reason to use the sweat is for the initiation of a young boy upon entering manhood. The men would counsel him on how to do a sweat correctly and tell him not to listen to false stories his young friends told him. He would be given as many chances as he needed to endure the sweat lodge ceremony. When a boy enters manhood, he cannot turn back. This could scare many a young heart because he now becomes responsible for his actions as a man. He will then learn to hunt to provide for his family and future wife. It is one thing to fish or kill a rabbit for food, but very difficult to hunt and kill a deer, turkey, or bear.

The second reason for a man to use the sweat is before entering marriage. This would ensure his mind and body were clean of all bad thoughts and make him pure for his mate. This gives the man time to think about whether he is making the right choice to marry.

The third reason is to mourn a mate, a child, a family member, an animal, or a friend who have either moved away or died. A man could openly express all his emotions or grief without scaring the children of the village. If a man cries in public, it was not considered a weakness but a sign he truly loved that person. The only time a man would not cry out was if an enemy was torturing him in public.

The fourth reason is to prepare for a hunt or battle. The man would use the sweat to take away all impurities and bodily odors. The animal's strong sense of smell could detect any strong bodily odor. Remember in those days, during the hunt, a man stood about six to twelve feet away from his prey.

The fifth reason is to remove illness from your body or mind. In the healing sweat, it is important not to dehydrate yourself. You need to drink water mixed with herbs to help you heal. The heat of the sweat and the herbal treatment triggers the immune system to bring about the healing process. When the person is removed from the sweat, they should be wrapped in a blanket and cooled down slowly. A cloth should be placed over their face so they do not breathe the outside air around him too fast. Once the immune system has been triggered, his own breath acts as a vaccine, and he will never get that illness again.

The sixth reason is to help him on a spiritual journey. A spiritual sweat is always done alone because the person is seeking the Great Spirit. The sweat lodge would let the man confront his fears and clear his mind of any doubt. He would sweat before going on a vision quest. Many men contact their spirit guide in the sweat. Some can only have visions in the sweat lodge.

Wetuomenese: the Women's Sweat

Women have a special lodge for their moon cycle. It can only be used during the times when she is menstruating and not by woman who no longer menstruate or has passed menopause. Women should not do a sweat if they are in moon time. This is not a good idea. You do it after moon time.

First, the sweat provides the relaxation, warmth, and relief from cramps and other discomforts.

Second is to mourn the loss of a mate, a child, a family member, an animal, or a friend who had either moved away or died. The reason for this is the woman prepares the body after death by washing and dressing it for burial. She needs to purify herself after handling the dead body.

Third is to prepare for a hunt or battle. Some women go on the hunt or go into battle with the men. They need to use the sweat before the hunt or battle to cleanse themselves of any odors. Yes, there are female warriors and hunters in the tribe.

The fourth reason is to remove illness from the body. The women use the same techniques as the men except for one big difference: all women are connected to Mother Earth. When a woman lays or walks on the ground, she automatically feels one with Mother Earth.

The fifth reason is to go on a spiritual journey. A woman does not have to do a spiritual sweat because every step she takes on Mother

Earth rejuvenates her. When a woman goes on a spiritual journey, she resists sexual temptations much easier than a man. When a man goes on a journey, the spirits can distract him with a beautiful young woman. A man has the primal instinct to respond sexually to a young female body that is of childbearing age. The woman doesn't have the sexual need to respond to any man. The medical profession and society keep insisting that a woman has a biological clock keeps ticking until you become menopausal. Men put the idea in a woman's head she must bear his children to prove she is a woman. Without the myth and the propaganda, women could care less. The sweat reminds the woman she is connected to Mother Earth.

Places for a Sweat

When finding a place to build a sweat, you need to make it right for you and not right for someone else. It should be a place where you will not be disturbed for at least two hours. Someone should be there to stand guard to stop anyone from interrupting or bothering you. Another person needs to be there to take care of the fire to heat up the rocks and bring the rocks inside the sweat. Be sure the firepit and the sweat are not close to anything that can catch fire.

The mountains are the place where many tribes would do a sweat. Please be careful about doing a sweat in your own backyard. Many communities have laws requiring a fire permit for an open fire. If possible, the native community might let you use their sweat if they have one. Just use common sense when picking your spot.

How to Build a Sweat Lodge

In the event there is no one to teach you, then use my guidelines for the sweat. If you are not native, then go with the direction you were born on the medicine wheel.

I use thirteen poles to represent the thirteen moons. When you build a sweat, remember, you are building the womb of Mother Earth. First, you smudge yourself then the area, the tools, firewood, water, and anything you are going to use to build the sweat. Once this is done, you are ready.

The sweat door should face east because this is where Father Sun rises, and we are the people of the morning light. The sweat and fire are shaped in a circle. The rocks will totally surround the sweat and the fire for the sweat. This shape is call the "squash," and the southwestern tribes call this the "rattle."

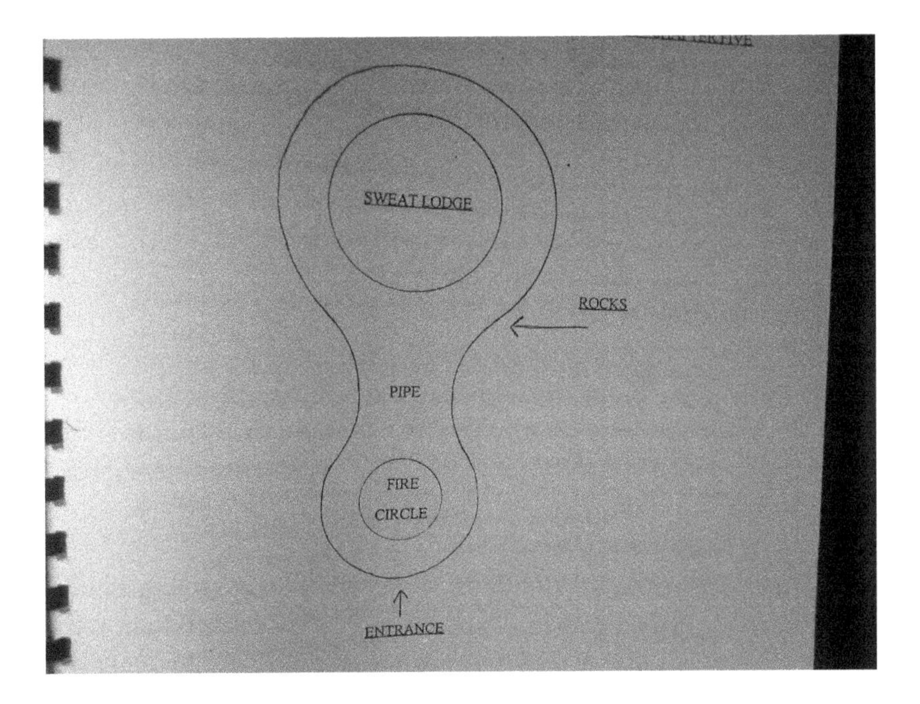

When you first set up the poles up, you start with the east side, then go to the south, west and last north. Many people set up a tripod first and add the poles onto that as long as the number comes out to thirteen. If you complete your sweat lodge and the number is twenty, seventeen, don't worry, it was meant to be built that way, you are not of a native nation. I have no choice; the sweat must be built with thirteen poles. The sweat should be in a dome shape and not a point.

Once you have the frame work up, sit in the fire circle spot in the sweat lodge and burn some sweetgrass, sage or the herb of your choice. If the sweat does not feel right to you, then take it down. The frame is the skeleton of the lodge and if that doesn't feel right then the rest will not work for you. If you have a broken bone in your leg, you cannot walk. The same idea applies to the lodge, the skeleton must feel right and be strong. The lodge frame will be supporting about one hundred to two hundred pounds of weight.

Once your frame work is done, you decide what materials you use to keep the heat in with. The one I suggest is buffalo hide, but you are looking at a heavy skin. The price of a buffalo hide is out of the reach for the average person.

I sewed together five deerskins and laid them on top of the lodge. After I cover the lodge with the skin, I take a heavy quilt or mover's blanket and lay that on top of the deerskins. Once I have done this, I put a plastic tarp over it to make sure no damage can come to the lodge.

Many natives will disagree with me for using plastic, but as my father would say: "If our ancestors had a plastic tarp, they would have used it." If the natives want to stay with tradition, then let them walk and not drive their smelly automobiles. We have the tools to improve the seat lodge and our lives, let's begin to use them wisely and stop disagreeing about improvements.

If you cannot build a lodge or if you are having someone build one for you, buy a new dome shaped tent. Many people do not want to cut a willow branch or a tree that bends; instead they use tentpoles that can make a dome shape. The problem with the tentpoles, they cannot support the heavy weight.

There are many books on the market on how to build a sweat lodge. Don't be afraid to try different ideas about how to build one. Remember, do and use whatever feels right for you. If you don't have enough animal skins to cover the sweat lodge, then just put it directly where you will be sitting in the lodge. Plastic tarps are cheap enough and come in various colors (camouflage).

Montauk Builds a Sweat Lodge for Waumausu

This is a story about a man who didn't believe in Pukwudgies and how he became a believer. He also learned how his love for a little girl named Waumausu, who believed in Pukwudgies, saved her life.

Many moons ago, when people still believed in magic, there was an Algonquian man named Montauk who did not believe in the twin giants, Maushop and his evil brother, Matahdou. They were the sons of the Great Creator named Kiehtan.

Whenever the village people talked about Pukwudgies turning into mosquitoes and biting them or stealing their corn, Montauk would tell them there were no such things as Pukwudgies. Pukwudgies are nasty, ugly and mean-spirited fairies; gremlins the natives believe in. They would steal babies, push people off cliffs and do many other evil things. Many of them were also swallowed by Mother Earth for their evil deeds and lived beneath the earth with Matahdou. Sometimes they would sneak up to the surface of the earth to do mischief.

Every day villagers would hear Montauk complaining about something that was wrong. They would tell him the Pukwudgies were bothering him. They told him to go to the Great Creator or Maushop for help. Montauk couldn't stand hearing any more stories about the Pukwudgies, so he decided to leave and live all alone outside of the village. The only friend he had in the village was a little girl who saw his good heart and brought him strawberry, blueberry, or cranberry bread when they were in season. She didn't want Montauk to leave because she would miss him. He told her he would be just beyond the path outside the village so that she could call to him when she wanted to visit. Montauk built his *wetu* (home), but he didn't know he had chosen a place near where the earth opens up.

One day the little girl brought him strawberry bread. He wanted to give the little girl a name. He thought for a long time and decided her name would be "Waumausu," which means "loving." When she came back after gathering firewood, he shared with her the name he had picked for her and she thanked him. She went back into the woods to gather more firewood, and it was then she felt the earth shake and tremble. She heard a loud noise and turned around as the earth opened up and swallowed her friend Montauk. She dropped the wood she held in her hands and ran back to the village to tell the people what happened.

Waumausu was crying so hard it took time before she could speak.

"Mother Earth swallowed Montauk and his wetu!" she cried.

The people of the village said, "That is what happened when Matahdou disappeared."

"We have to save Montauk!" Waumausu cried.

"There is nothing we can do, child," said her mother.

Waumausu said Montauk had given her a name and it was Waumausu.

"That is a good name he gave you," said her mother. "From now on, you will be known as Waumausu."

Waumausu picked flowers and put them on the spot where Montauk's lodge once stood. "I will miss you," she cried. Every week she left flowers and a bowl of food for Montauk in the same spot. The next day when she returned, the flowers and the bowl of food mysteriously disappeared.

What Waumausu didn't know was that Montauk had tumbled head over heels down beneath the earth, lower and lower and lower and lower until he finally hit the ground so hard he almost couldn't breathe. The only thing that saved him was that he landed on several small lodges which broken his fall. They were about twelve inches high and made out of twigs and grass. He was so dazed he couldn't get up and thought he was seeing things. As he stood up he couldn't imagine who could possibly be this small. He thought he could hear little voices around him, but he was so jostled by the fall he fell asleep.

When he awoke, his whole body was so stiff and sore he could hardly move. He looked up and saw a cave nearby that looked larger than any other cave he had seen before. He heard a little voice saying, "Go into the lodge. Go into the sweat lodge, it will heal you."

Montauk listened to the voice and slowly crawled over to the sweat lodge and went inside. It was very hot in there after the flap closed. Every once in a while he would see a little hand pour water on the hot rocks to create steam.

After a while, the pain began to go away as his body sweat more and more inside the lodge. A little voice said, "It is time for you to leave the sweat lodge and wash your body."

When he left the lodge, he saw a small waterfall with new clothes lying beside it. There were plants and herbs to wash with. After Montauk had washed and dressed in his new clothes, he felt so good he realized he was hungry. He looked over and saw a bowl of food on the rocks.

As he sat there eating the food, he said, "Who are you? Show yourselves, I am known as Montauk. Who are you?"

He heard giggling and laughter around him and thought about what Waumausu had told him. He asked, "Are you Pukwudgies?"

They came forward and said, "That is who we are."

"Where did you get the food? It tastes like the food Waumausu used to bring me, but that cannot be," said Montauk.

"Yes, it can," giggled the Pukwudgies. "She has been leaving you food every week at the place where you were swallowed by the Mother Earth. We have been saving all the food we could for you to eat. We must warn you, there is one place where you may not go," the Pukwudgies told Montauk.

"Where is that?" he asked. "And why?"

The Pukwudgies pointed to a huge cave and said, "That is Matahdou's cave. You must not go there or make him angry, or he will step on you, crush you, and squeeze you until your eyeballs pop out! That is what he does to us!"

Montauk kept thinking he had to be dreaming. "You can't be real," he said to the Pukwudgies.

"But we are," they said as they took their little arrows and began jabbing him all over his body.

"Ouch!" Montauk cried. "Those feel just like mosquitoes."

Time went by and Montauk would share the food Waumausu left for him each week. He would leave strawberry bread outside of Matahdou's cave. One day Montauk asked the Pukwudgies to find him a piece of leather when they went about the ground so he could make Waumausu a pair of moccasins to thank her for the food she had given him.

The next day, they brought him the leather, and he made the moccasins. The Pukwudgies left the moccasins for Waumausu and watched as Waumausu found them and hugged them.

For years, she still thought about Montauk and left him food each week because she knew he was alive and living below the earth. Montauk sent little presents to Waumausu through the Pukwudgies. Many years passed, and the Pukwudgies came to Montauk in dismay.

"You must come with us up above because Waumausu is sick."

"How do you know she is sick?" questioned Montauk.

"When we went to get the food, there wasn't anything there. We went to her long house. We found her ill and told her we would bring you to her. You can help her!" said the Pukwudgies.

"How can I get up there to get to her village? I am not small like you," said Montauk. They thought for a while and the Pukwudgies had an idea.

"You can go to Matahdou. Maybe he will help you. He can bring you above the earth if he wants to," they told Montauk.

He slowly approached the cave and called out to the giant Matahdou. Matahdou told Montauk to go away. Montauk explained he had to go above the earth to help Waumausu who brought him food or she could die. He yelled back, "Let her die!"

Montauk told Matahdou he would not leave him any more strawberry bread if he would not bring him to Waumausu. Matahdou thought for a while, because he really loved strawberry bread. He agreed to bring Montauk to Waumausu at great risk to himself.

What Montauk did not know was if Matahdou was caught above the earth, he would be put on a star far, far away.

Matahdou put Montauk in his pouch and began to climb to the surface. As Montauk was being tossed around in the pouch, he hoped he could trust Matahdou to bring him to the surface. Suddenly, Matahdou came to a stop and the pouch was opened up. Sunlight rushed in and stung Montauk's eyes. Before he knew what had happened, Montauk tumbled to the ground as Matahdou tipped open his pouch.

As Montauk stood up, the Pukwudgies cried, "Come this way, hurry, follow us!"

Montauk ran and tried to keep up with the Pukwudgies. The people in the village recognized him and were surprised to see him surrounded by Pukwudgies. Everyone pointed to where the girl's long house was. He went in and looked at her and knew what to do.

He left the long house and told the villagers: "I am Montauk. I am going to teach you how to build a sweat lodge to help the girl."

The villages followed his directions and built a sweat lodge. He put the girl inside the sweat and had a medicine woman watch over her. He told the medicine woman how to help the girl.

Time passed and the girl recovered. She came out and looked up at Montauk and said, "I knew you would come to help me." The village people thanked him for showing them how to build a medicine sweat lodge. Montauk knew it was time to go below, and he asked for some strawberry bread to bring to Matahdou. When he arrive at the spot where he was to meet Matahdou the Pukwudgies said, "He was being punished for disobeying his father."

Montauk had to save Matahdou. He gathered all the people of the village to ask them to help Matahdou. When the people gathered in a circle, they prayed to Kishtannit and their ancestors. They told Kiehtan Matahdou was helping the little girl get better and he had done no wrong. Kiehtan knew this, and decided to send Matahdou back on one condition: he must never leave the island in the bay (Martha's Vineyard). Montauk and a small group of people decided to live on the island with Matahdou. The people were happy, and Montauk had new friends and old. He did not have to live below the earth anymore.

Chapter Seven

Vision Quest

Today, there are several reasons for a vision quest if you are not a medicine person: to get in touch with your spiritual and physical body. You can ask one hundred people what a vision quest is, and you will get one hundred different answers. I'm sure someone who has been on a vision quest will either agree or disagree with what I am about to say: "Seventy-five percent of vision quests today are phony!"

The name "vision quest" is very misleading. I've always called it "having a private talk with the Great Creator" or "getting my life back on track." It is a time for you to be alone with your thoughts, feelings, emotions, body, and spiritual self. It is one of the important religious rituals of the Native American Indian people. It is one of the few times when you come face to face with your spirit helper, guide, ancestors, and your God.

Going on a vision quest should not be the "in thing" to do. I keep reading in the New Age magazines: "Vision Quests from three-hundred to one-thousand dollars. We take credit cards." Native American Indian spirituality is being raped by non-natives. It is not for sale! Beware of people who charge for a vision quest. Check into their background. This is dangerous in the wrong hands.

The other line that irritates me is they conduct "workshops" and "special classes," all for a very high price. I can hear some of you screaming, "Hypocrite! Aren't you selling your book to make money?" I reply, "Yes, but I'm not charging you three hundred to one thousand dollars for my book."

I find people who brag about how many certificates they have to teach a vision quest to be amusing. I didn't know you needed a certificate to teach about a vision quest. Many of the Medicine Women I have met never made it past the third grade, they taught me how to do a vision quest just fine. As Many Names, who received her doctorate from Harvard said, "The bigger the words and higher initials after their name, the larger the ass they are!"

Many people who go on a vision quest never have a vision because not everyone is meant to have a vision. This does not mean you did something wrong. I can't sing opera; does that mean I did something wrong? I don't have the voice to do so. My spirit guide is there to protect me even if it means for me not to have a vision.

Geronimo (One Who Yawns) was a holy man who would go on many vision quests to find answers for his people. This was a time when he needed to know the answers to the decisions he had to make. He was told in a vision he had to surrender, and the United States government was lying to him about the terms of the surrender. He knew that it had to be.

Crazy Horse was another holy man who went on many vision quests to find answers for his people. He knew when he was going to die and how. He told his people an Indian would stab him in the back to kill him. When he was dying, he made several predictions and many have come true.

Weetamoe, the Warrior Queen of the Pocasset Tribe and the Pokanoket Nation, had many visions about her people and what was to come. She knew she could not change the future, but she was going to kill as many English men and women she could before she died. She knew her brother-in-law, Metacom (King Philip), was going to set a trap for her to die. She never turned her back on him.

These people and more had a purpose for a vision quest: to help their people and to gain knowledge. Today, people go on a vision quest for selfish reasons, it's just another new gimmick to try.

A woman does not need to go on a vision quest because she is a natural transmitter for information from Mother Earth. Men are not connected to Mother Earth but to Father Sky. They need help in seeking visions; they need to starve their physical bodies and shock their minds.

Places for a Vision Quest

The first thing you need to do when choosing a place to have your vision quest is to use common sense. What does the place do for you? Don't think of what books tell you or what your friends might think is right, but what works for you.

Today, people do not go out in fear of being attacked or worse. This is why the place you pick should be safe for you and the people with you. Sitting on the edge of a high cliff and putting yourself and others in danger is the wrong approach.

Remember, a polar bear cannot survive in Hawaii or a hummingbird in the arctic; the place must be right for you. If someone is trying to talk you into going to their spot, go; it just might work for you. If it doesn't, tell them it was not right for you. If they should become angry with your answer, ask them to help you find your special spot.

First, find a place inside or outside where you will not be disturbed. Your bedroom, bathroom, living room, or library. A state or national forest, the roof of a building, park, boat, beach, desert, or mountain make excellent locations for a vision quest. Many people feel more comfortable in their own church, synagogue, temple, mosque, or other religious buildings. As a church organist, I have done my most spiritual writing in church while the sermon was being said.

I have several vision quest places which my people use when they need an answer to a problem. The mountain we go to depends on the question. Potumtuck (Mount Hope) is the place to find out about the past, Mount Wachusetts for the present, and Mount Monadnock for the future. There are special places I go to help someone or myself in a spiritual or physical healing.

Many people experience visions and they think they are just day dreaming. If the Great Spirit wants you to be aware of a situation, he will send you a vision wherever you are. This means you could be walking down the street and see or hear something. Just before you fall asleep or wake up, you could have a vision and call it a vivid dream. Write down your dreams or use a tape recorder, you might find out you are having visions in your twilight sleep about your life or a situation.

How to Go on a Vision Quest

Before you decide to go on a vision quest, you have to know why you want to go on one. Do you need a question answered or something has been bothering you a long time? Do you have an illness you cannot find the reason for? Do you want to heal yourself? Are you seeking spiritual knowledge? Are you emotionally troubled? I advise you to seek the answers to one question at a time on your vision quest. The reason for this is if you ask three questions, you will get three different answers. You won't know which answer goes with what question.

There are many ways to prepare for a vision quest, some are simple and others are extreme. Going on a vision quest is not a game you should play, neither should you go to the extreme of harming your body, mind, or spirit. In order for the vision to be successful, you should be sincere about your feelings. Please do not embark upon a vision quest if you have any doubts. The vision quest is similar to marriage but with two big differences: there is no divorce, and death enhances the vision quest experience. One of the purposes of a vision quest is to prepare you for your own death, but that does not mean that a vision quest should be used to commit suicide. Many people have starved themselves on a vision quest, both in the past and in the present.

If you choose to use your home or apartment, unplug all the electrical appliances, especially the telephone. If you can, shut your breakers to stop the electrical current in the room you will be in. Try to eliminate any distraction that might bother you. Find a babysitter or pet-sitter to leave your child or pet with so you can have total concentration. If you can't get a babysitter, wait for everyone to go to sleep then try your meditation. Please do not shut off your home or fire alarm system.

Some people cannot find their own space. If you cannot, ask a friend to help you. If it doesn't work, then find a place in a new age magazine that specializes in doing vision quests. I do not encourage this, because it is not the native way to charge money for religious ceremonies.

Decide what offerings you are going to give and what you are going to place them in. When you are done, bring the offering outside to leave for Mother Earth. Once you have found a place to have your vision quest, you are ready to prepare your body, mind, and spirit for your journey.

If you are serious about preparing your body for a vision quest, you might find it very difficult to get through the initial stage of sticking to a strictly vegetarian diet for twenty-eight days (moon cycle) beforehand. That means you should abstain from *any* meat, poultry, or fish during this time. Also abstain from eating fried foods, candy, most junk foods, carbonated beverages, and most important of all, *no* alcohol or narcotics (drugs).

You should begin your twenty-eight days of preparation by eating three full meals a day. Gradually, cut your food intake down to the point where each meal consists of only as much as you can fit in the palm of your hand or one cup. Your palm is supposed to be the size of your natural stomach, and do not eat less than that because it would be dangerous.

If you have any medical problems such as diabetes, heart or other serious problems, please use common sense. I suggest you tell the person who is running the vision quest about your health problems to better accommodate you.

One of the problems I see with the paid vision quest is they believe you only fast when you are on the vision quest. They do not allow for preparation ahead of time and many of them do not ask about your physical, spiritual, or mental health.

During the twenty-eight days of preparation, your body has been cleansing itself of toxins and your body might react to it by shaking. I call this the DTs (detoxification). Your awareness will be heightened to the point you will feel a glass of water going down your esophagus. You are preparing your body physically for your vision quest my minimizing your food intake and eliminating unhealthy and toxic foods from your diet. You must also prepare your mind. While you are cleansing your body, you should also cleanse your mind. The time you choose to do your vision quest is very important. The Native Americans believe if it is your time to do a vision quest, you need to make any arrangements necessary to accomplish this. Anyone can be replaced, no matter how hard it may seem. You can find a way to make the time if you really want to. If you don't think you can take the time to do this, you are not ready.

You might wonder how it is possible to cleanse your mind. Try starting out by not using obscene language. Replace offensive language with more positive speech. I met a man who is a drummer at a powwow named Travis. He corrected me on a word I used to describe a person. I promised him I would never use that word again and I have not. Gear your mind toward a more positive way of thinking and speaking. If you do, please refrain from reading or viewing pornographic books and films.

Limit your television and movie viewing to no more than one hour a day. Eliminate violent programs and the news. Select programs such as comedies that will make you laugh or neutral educational or nature programs. Avoid being over stimulated by modern technology. This means cutting back not only on television viewing but video games, listening to rock music, e-mail, radio, the internet, cell phones, and general personal computer use.

In preparing for a vision quest, you are trying to clear your mind of excessive clutter and overstimulation so you can reach a peaceful and meditative state of mind. You need to prepare your mind to pray. Television programming and their commercials emphasize and suggest sex, materialism, and illness in a very powerful way. The public is bombarded with the media's propaganda. The message is delivered is: buy, be sexually attractive, take a pill. Do anything it takes to be young, beautiful, healthy and rich. Unfortunately, there is a wealth of information that can be received through television and no other means. It becomes necessary to take the bad along with the good to get the information you really want and need. Watching television is taking one or two aspirins, a little bit is fine, but a whole bottle might kill you. Commercials encourage you to be ill: got a problem? Take a pill.

Prayer is the most ancient form of spiritual communication known to mankind. Some people like to recite prayers that are written in a structured religious format, others like to write their own prayers. Some people like to pray spontaneously by talking to their God. Sadly enough, there are people who feel they are incapable of praying, and they make excuses for why they cannot pray. Often they feel there is no God to pray to. God believes in you; you are not a mistake.

If the Great Spirit is not used to hearing your voice in prayer, you don't always get the answer you want. Sometimes the answer is no. I like to thank the Great Spirit for my past, present, and future blessings. "Ah-ho!"

If you feel your life is too complicated and you have too many responsibilities, then you should reevaluate your life. The spirits have their own way of making you slow down. If your body, mind, and spirit get together and force you to slow down, you will. Carpal tunnel syndrome, a broken leg, sprained ankle, migraine headaches, ulcers, heart attacks, strokes are all examples of what your body, mind, and spirit might bring about. The ultimate example of ignoring an illness would be death.

When you are on a vision quest, you are considered "dead" to the outside world because you have no idea of what is going on around you. The only way people can have a vision is if they are just about to go to sleep or if they are in a deep sleep. This is fine if it is a naturally induced sleep, but if you use artificial means to induce sleep, you are only adding toxins to your body. For example, melatonin tablets taken for sleep can give you bad dreams and nightmares. You can wake up feeling sluggish and unresponsive. This is not to be confused with a natural herb such as chamomile, which has a gentle calming effect. I drink Yogi stress tea mixed with Sleeping time. Works for me.

Do not confuse a vision quest with astral projection (out-of-body experiences). During a vision quest experience your body, mind, and spirit as one, there is no separation. The reason is, you have to prepare your body, mind, and spirit before you go on a vision quest. People have been known to have no problems cleansing their bodies and their minds for the twenty-eight days before a vision quest. For whatever the reason, they have trouble cleansing their spirit ahead of time.

If you have trouble meditating, focusing, and concentrating, you will have trouble doing a vision quest. You have to go deep within yourself. The way you know your spirit needs cleansing is by picturing an object in your mind in different colors. Think of the object to represent your spirit, a rainbow, a ball, a box, a stone. Does it need cleaning or repairing? If it does, clean it or repair it until it is shiny and new. Your body, mind, and spirit will not join together unless they are all purified first.

You're probably asking yourself if there is another way to cleanse your spirit because the method I suggested didn't work for you. How I see if my spirit needs repair is the rainbow method. This is when you visualize a rainbow and clean and repair each color. Picture one crescent at a time. If any color is dirty, clean it until it is beautiful again. After I completed my cleaning, I walk into the rainbow and become one with the colors. Many people have written several books on this subject. Many people go on a vision quest do not think they are having a vision or had one but they did in their conscious, subconscious, and unconscious states. There is a Pokanoket term to describe these terms; we call it "deconscious."

You never know when your vision or the knowledge from the vision will come into your mind. Some people never know in their life until the time just before they die. Their vision here was to help them before death and not when they were living on earth. One day friends and I were at a campfire. We were talking about some really strange subjects. Many of them came up with theories that were astounding, and profound. We would all look at each other and said, wow, that knowledge you just shared was from your vision quest or meditation stored in the back of your mind.

When you do pick your friends to watch over you, keep a journal. Please be careful on your choice of friends. You don't want a person who is frightened by a leaf falling from a tree or one who will think you are dead and rush over and disturb your vision. Explain to them what you are doing and ask them to record how they were feeling and what they saw or heard.

Step-by-Step

1. Know why you are going on this vision quest and try to only ask one question.
2. Choose your location. If inside, stop all electrical current in the room, especially the telephone. Please do not shut off your home or fire alarm system.
3. Smudge yourself and start your twenty-eight days of cleansing and prayer.
4. Smudge everything you are going to use in the vision quest, including the stick and rope. Smudge the area you are about to use.
5. Draw a circle in the dirt or sand to mark your area. If you cannot do this, then put a rope or tape to mark your circle.
6. Place the blanket on the floor and place your offering on it. If you need a chair, then use a table to put your offering on it. Give an offering to each direction.
7. Place your offerings either on your blanket or table.
8. Light your sage, sweetgrass, or whatever smudge you are using and smudge yourself.
9. Get into a meditative state and relax your body. Ask your question and wait for your vision.

10. Have one or two friends stay at a distance from you (at least twenty feet away) so no one disturbs or disrupts you. Have the people there keep a journal on what is happening around you and them.
11. You should not go longer than three days of meditation.
12. Slowly awaken from your vision and move around at a leisurely pace.
13. Gradually return to eating more food at each meal.
14. Keep a personal journal (or use a tape recorder) to record everything happening to you.
15. Don't be surprised if you don't understand what your vision means, you will find out what it means in due time; you did in your "deconscious" state.

Amerindian Legend: Seven Sisters in the Sky

Many moons ago, there were nine sisters in the sky. They were jealous of their sister, Mother Earth. She had beautiful blue waters, purple mountains, and green valleys. Two sisters were so jealous they lied to their other sisters about what sister Earth had said. All seven sisters got together and bumped into sister Earth. Sister Mother Earth cried out, "Why are you hurting me?"

The sisters kept bumping into her, making her oceans go over the land and causing many problems. Sister Earth prayed to the Great Creator to help her. When five of the sisters heard her cries to the Great Creator, they stopped because they understood what they were doing was wrong. But two wanted to keep bumping, as they were getting enjoyment watching the oceans and land move violently. As the sisters gave her one last bump, several large pieces flew into the sky and the Great Creator caught them. He looked down on the sisters. He was very disappointed.

Then he spoke: "Who is to blame for this needless destruction?"

The Moon came forward and told the Great Creator all that had happened and wished to apologize to Sister Earth for not helping her. The Great Creator gathered all the pieces in the sky that had broken away from Earth and the other sisters.

The Great Creator pointed at the two most jealous sisters and said, "As punishment, you will be the farthest from your sisters. You both will be hidden by the Sun. You will no longer look upon your sister Earth."

Then he looked at the third sister he had asked to pick up all the pieces. "You [Saturn] will live with rings of pieces of your sisters around your head as a reminder not to destroy someone you love."

He turned to the fourth sister and said, "You [Jupiter] who are the largest will watch over your other sister. You will keep their place in the sky and never to harm sister Earth again."

He turned and pointed at the fifth sister. "You [Mars] will have saltwater on your land to remind you the tears your sister Earth cried."

He turned to the sixth sister who was jealous of sister Earth's aroma. "You [Venus] will be surrounded with toxic odors, no one will want to come near you."

The Great Creator stood there looking at the seventh sister. He decided to put this sister next to Father Sun. He looked at Father Sun and said, "Father Sun, this sister [Mercury] will not turn for you but stay still as a reminder of how she was silent and did not help sister Mother Earth. She will be hot on one side and cold on the other."

Last, he called the eighth sister and named her Grandmother Moon. "You apologized to sister Mother Earth, you will follow closest to your sister. You will give Father Sun light and shine on her. You will follow Father Sun and never complete a circle around sister Mother Earth. You will stand still in the Grandfather Sky and sister Earth will always go before you." (For one day after every twenty-eight days, the moon cannot be seen after a full moon.)

The Great Creator looked at Father Sun and said, "You will be the center, and everyone will dance around you. If the sisters should fight again, destroy them."

Father Sun nodded in agreement. The Great Creator looked at sister Earth in his hands and became sad.

"Why are you sad, Great Creator?" said sister Mother Earth.

"I am sad because people will never learn to respect you as I have. I give you the power to shake yourself. I give you the power to call the winds at your command and push your water against the land. I give you power of having your mountains spit fire and smoke to release your anger."

He turned to everyone in the sky and said, "Let it be known that from now on sister Earth will be called 'Mother Earth.'"

Eileen's First Vision

The week started out no different from any other week, but things changed as the weekend approached. My friends decided to take me out, and we stayed out all night having a good time. I was the designated driver, but I came home around three in the morning. I only had one hour to take a shower, get dressed, and catch the bus for the airport. There is nothing worse than sitting on a bus with a headache, no sleep, and everything spinning endlessly around you. When I looked out the window at the road, it made things worse. I felt as if I was being sucked into a vortex. By the time I got to Boston, I looked like a dishrag. My tongue was swollen, my eyes puffy red, and I was white as a ghost. I could just about put my suitcase on the weigh-in platform. The airline clerk wanted to know if I needed any help. I feebly said "No" and shuffled off to have a seat in the lobby. Everything felt safe as I sat in my chair waiting until a family with a screaming four-year-old child came along ready to board the plane.

I thought, *I will sleep on the plane*. Unfortunately for me, they boarded the same plane and were next to me all the way to Arizona.

After being in flight with a screaming child, the plane landed in Arizona, the screech of the tires hitting the ground felt like nails scratching across a blackboard in my head and ears. The ladies were there waiting for me in the lobby to take me to the mission house. When I got out of the truck and shuffled up to the porch, they told me to sit down. Many Names looked at me and said, "Did you fast for twenty-eight days?"

I answered, "Yes."

She folded her arms in front of her and stared at me. She looked around at the other medicine women and they all nodded their heads back at her.

"This is a good time for a vison quest," Many Names said. I nodded my head in agreement. I looked at the merciless faces of the medicine women, and a cold chill went down my back.

From that moment on, they started to prepare me for my vision quest journey. I went to bed early with a bad headache from the lack of sleep and the child screaming on the plane. The medicine women promised to be considerate of my headache; I thought I was going to get a decent night sleep.

Before sunrise, I was rudely awakened by the sound of drumming and chanting. I put the pillow over my head and refused to give in to their immature behavior and my own childish impulse to get up to put a hole in the drum. Oddly enough the pounding in my head sometimes matched the drumbeat.

My head was still pounding, and my throat was still sore from being sick. After getting a glass of water, I walked over to the medicine women sitting in a circle on the porch. I asked what the drumming had been about when they knew I had gone to bed with a bad headache. They stopped shucking the corn and looked at me as innocently as possible for them.

"We were sending you healing energies," they replied.

I looked at them with disgust and said, "I don't believe you all for a second!"

They all burst out laughing, which prompted Many Names to say, "Well, time for a vision quest."

One of the medicine women went into the house and came out with water and a choice of dried fruit, raisin and nut mix for food for the journey. I picked the raisin and nut mix and took the water. Before dawn in the morning light, we started to walk in an easterly direction. The desert air was crisp and cool as it touched my skin. It felt good on my head and face. We finally reached our destination, I laid out my blanket, ceremonial pipe, and offerings to greet the sunrise.

"We will be watching you in case you need our help," Many Names said as they walked away from my spot.

As I sat there and lit my sage bowl, I noticed how the sky slowly changed from black to dark blue to light blue as the Sun peaked up from the mountaintops. There is nothing more beautiful than a sunrise in the Southwest. The brilliant colors totally overtake you as the rays of sunlight reach out to touch you. The first sliver of the sunlight brought out these tiny little insects that seemed to be awakening all the animal life in the desert. As each ray of the sun appeared, my headache began to go away. The sun started to heat the morning air and dry the dampness of the night. My skin tingled and began to warm up.

I lit my pipe, gave my offering, and said my morning prayer. As I sat there on my special spot with my eyes closed, I began to think I was never going to have a vision. I kept looking at my wrist to see the time, but they took my watch away from me. I didn't realize how much I relied upon my stochastic model of chronological sequence (a watch). I began to using my mind to think of a way to tell how much time had passed. Looking for clues, time seemed to be dragging, almost standing still. I stood up to look at my shadow. An idea came to me. I made a circle in the sand and place a rock on the edge of my shadow as a time marker. I felt very proud of myself. I stepped out of the circle and looked at my little creation feeling smug. I laid on my blanket in the circle, fell asleep feeling confident that I had solved the time dilemma. When I awoke, I stood in the circle on my footprints, looked down, the shadow was in the exact same position as it was when I fell asleep.

"Did I sleep for twenty-four hours?" What happened? I was totally baffled. I got out of the circle, drank some water, and ate a handful of raisin-and-nut mix. I scratched my head and tried to figure it out. Had my clever scheme backfired on me?

As I stood there looking at the circle, out of the corner of my eye, I saw one of my animal helpers. I thought, *This is good. She is here to help me.*

Boy, was I wrong. The next thing I knew, all my animal helpers were showing up and surrounding me. An uneasy feeling came over me, I wished I had not started on a vision quest. I looked around frantically for the medicine women but they were nowhere to be found.

"We will be watching you in case you need our help," I said out loud in a mocking voice. "Where are they?"

I thought, *Don't panic. See what the animals want first, then panic.*

One by one each animal helper approached me; making eye contact, speaking to me in their own language which I amazingly understood. As each animal accomplished want it was supposed to say to me, it returned to its place in the circle. This went on until all the animals gave me their message and healing. I kept thinking, *Where are the medicine women?*

It was at this point I realized my animal helpers gave me many messages, healings and a new start on my medicine path. I thanked the animals, lit my sage and gave them an offering.

The sun was hot against my skin as I crawled over for my water jug. I leaned back on one arm and poured the water over my head and into my mouth. I collapsed and went into a deep sleep. When I opened my eyes, I was surrounded in the circle of medicine women standing in the place where the animals stood. In my mind, I wasn't sure which circle I would rather be in the middle of: the animals or the medicine women. I didn't understand it at the time, but later it helps you to listen to people more attentively without being self-absorbed. Your ability to empathize with people develops.

The medicine women stared at me. Some with their arms folded in front of them and others with their hands on their hips. Many Names spoke, "I see you had a vision." She held out her hand to help me up.

As we walked back to the house, I told the medicine women what had happened. Cornflower argued I had experienced sleep deprivation. Others argued I had a true vision and was on my way to helping others heal as well as myself. Many Names smiled.

Chapter Eight

The Spirit Medicine Wheel

The spiritual medicine wheel is simple: spiritual. You cannot physically touch it unless you are in a spiritual state. Like your spiritual medicine bag, there are no boundaries or limitations. What you wanted to do with your physical medicine wheel but couldn't, you can do with your spiritual wheel. You can create your spirit medicine wheel the same way you created your spirit medicine bag. You can even take objects from your spirit medicine bag to use in your spirit medicine wheel. Once you have your spirit medicine wheel in your mind, you can use it anytime you need it. You will find that in a crisis situation the spirit medicine wheel will pop into your mind. Some people use the spirit medicine wheel to help them understand things they are trying to learn. It makes your mind act like a sponge to absorb the information you are trying to learn. The spirit medicine wheel will never pop into your mind while you are driving or running machinery. The spirit medicine wheel will never put your life in danger or put you in a situation, which is wrong. Always remember to follow your dreams and seek fulfillment.

Before I type a word or turn on my computer, I smell sage or sweetgrass. Then I visualize my spirit medicine wheel. Once this was accomplished, I would turn on the computer, go to the chapter I was working on, and begin to type. The spirits guided my hands in writing all three medicine-wheel trilogies.

The spirit medicine wheel is a tool at your disposal, which you use at your free will. If you do not use it constructively, then you can or will destroy it. If you destroy it by accident or otherwise, you can rebuild it or make a new one. For example: Winona was working on her spirit wheel when she became discouraged. As soon as she said, "I can't do this, I wish it would go away," the wheel disappeared. There's that word "can't" again. Remove it from your vocabulary. If someone claims they can destroy your spirit wheel, do not believe them. Only you and you alone have that power.

First, sit down and set up your physical medicine wheel. When you look at your wheel, stare at it hard so when you close your eyes, you can still see it in your mind. This takes practice, time, and patience. Keep trying until you can do it. People with a photographic memory have no trouble doing this, but if you are like me, keep trying until you get it. You can train your mind to do this. Once you have accomplished this, go on to the next step. As I mentioned earlier, when you are outside the physical realm, you are as limited as your imagination.

By now you should have made your physical medicine wheel and decided on what animals are around it. It is not important to memorize what animal helpers are in what place because they constantly change.

Some people change their clans as I would my socks. You should decide what clan and totem goes in what position on your medicine wheel. If you think change is a good thing, think about what happens when a two-way street is changed to a one-way street. Change becomes dangerous in a situation if you are not aware. Are you one of those people who rearrange their furniture in your home every month? Make your spirit wheel feel right for you even if it takes years to complete it.

Spirit Mountain: "Mountain with No Name" or "Mirror Mountain"

Spirit Mountain represents the place where the Great Creator lives and cannot be found on the physical earth. Many people do not believe this mountain exists because they do not believe in the Great Creator or any God. The other reason is they have no faith in themselves or God, angels, or spirit guides to help them in this world.

Other people I have spoken with call it "Mirror Mountain" or the "Spirit Place above the mountain." The way you know you have arrived at this special place is you are one with God and you become all-knowing. This is not to be confused with a near-death experience. In a near-death experience, one or more things are happening to you: You might experience a negative or positive event or feeling; you will meet a relative or pet who has died or a family member who has died. Some people experience an inner peace and oneness with a bright light. This could almost be described as "Mirror Mountain," but it does not come close to what it is like to be one with the Great Spirit.

It is difficult, in these modern times, to ask someone to believe in something they cannot see, hear, or touch. Even when they do, sometimes they have doubt and will not believe. What I would like to do is bring you on a highly spiritual journey one step at a time. It can be the most profound spiritual experience you will ever have.

You are alone with the Great Spirit on "Mirror Mountain," it is just you and your God. The only light, bright white or any color that comes to you, comes from within you and not from the outside. It will be at this point you will have no negative energy or feelings within you. Then you will be given knowledge and wisdom beyond your understanding to use at a later time.

When people come back, many of them have a glow around their face and heads. They walk and talk differently because they are at peace with themselves and everyone. People call this "the Moses syndrome." When you become one, you do not leave your body and you are all-knowing. In my experience, I feel I am glowing from the inside out. People do see the difference in you.

When you do go to the mountains and come back, you might get a strong desire to do something. Do it! Please use common sense. Be sure what you attempt to do has been well-thought-out and planned ahead. You should know the routine by now, but in case you forgot, smudge yourself and the surrounding area. I have faith in the Great Spirit. I also know some people are not honest or moral. However, I try to give people the benefit of the doubt. When you return from Spirit Mountain, the feeling is even more illuminating.

You will do things differently and possess the courage to do things you always wanted to do. You see no barriers or roadblocks ahead, and when you wonder where you got the knowledge to do things you planned, you remember you went to Spirit Mountain. The inhibitions that stopped you before from doing the things in your heart's desire, "follow your bliss." It's good advice.

Footprints in the Sky

Do not confuse the information you store in your subconscious with "channeling." After leaving Spirit Mountain, information will slowly be released to you at the proper time. On more than one occasion, I have been asked where I got my information. I replied, "Spirit mountain." One person said it looked like I was "channeling information from the past or the future." I said, "No, they were wrong."

Channeling is not a new age discovery because indigenous people have been doing it since the beginning of time. I will not deny I channel information to help people, but when it pops into my head, that is spirit mountain's library coming to me.

We have "cultural amnesia"; I will break open the doors to let everyone in! Many of us have memory of the Star People, but we keep it hidden in our minds. I believe someone or something will trigger our amnesia causing us to have a thought that we put into action.

After this happens, we think to ourselves, *Where did this thought come from?*

Don Ousa Mequin calls this "genetic memory." He feels not everyone is from the Star People and many are from earth alone. This is why people who have the DNA of Star People do not have any difficulty going astral or meditation while others struggle. Think blood type O negative; only 15 percent of the people in the world and my mother is one. Many say this blood type is alien or Star People.

The Star People are the "Ancient Beings of Light." These ancient beings of light were approximately eight to twelve feet tall, with exceedingly smooth, luminescent skin, their faces almost like water that reflects they saw. I call this the mercury look.

The Native American Indian talked about their ancestors in the sky, and people laughed at them. The natives were in balance with nature and themselves until they had their land taken away from them and their culture destroyed.

I hope the *Medicine Wheel Trilogy* will help bring you back in balance with Mother Earth. Remember to honor Mother Earth and not repeat the mistakes of the past. Everything we do is a circle: if you are have having trouble with something from the past, look at the present, go forward, and when you come to the problem again, you will have the solution. You are never alone. Aquene peace.

Personal Story
Full Moon: Day of Truth!

When I first went to the medicine mission in Arizona, I had no idea how the medicine women altered the truth. It was the first time I was in Arizona for the full moon cycle, I was not aware or had no knowledge of the ancient tradition they practiced.

Two nights before full moon, the closer we walked to the fire circle, the faster they walked to get a seat next to the talking stick. Each tribe uses their own designs, size, and style for their talking stick. As one person sat down on the log, another would try to nudge her off the log. Once the fire was lit and prayers said, they began wrestling for the talking stick. The talking stick was passed around the circle to allow everyone to have a chance to speak. Only the person holding the stick was allowed to speak. When the person finished speaking, they would lay the stick in its special place. Before the stick even left the fingers of the person who was done talking, there was a mad dash to grab it.

I noticed Cornflower, Little Chipmunk and Night Wind did not grab for the talking stick for those two nights. They knew their chance would come. One at a time, each medicine women would get up and tell their "tall tale" about experiences with life, a vision quest, or the sweat lodge. Each time one of them got up to tell their story, they became more difficult to believe. At one point, Many Names turned to me after a woman sat down and said, "That one was really hard to swallow. How do they expect me to eat my dinner after those words?" She was saying this as we walked to the mission house. As the other medicine women were walking to dinner, they continued to try to outdo one another with their incredible stories.

The only time they stopped their bantering was when everyone stood around the table to thank the Creator for their meal and the one who cooked it. As they continued trying to outdo one another throughout the meal with their stories, Night Wind banged on the table with her fist and yelled: "Enough already!"

Dead silence filled the air. I looked at Many Names, and when she looked at my face, she said, "You really don't believe those stories do you?"

I sat there confused and bit my lip as the medicine women slowly continued with their stories again. That night Cornflower walked up to Night Wind and said, "Tomorrow is the start of the full moon."

Night Wind raised her hands in the air and yelled, "Hallelujah!"

We all picked our spots for sleeping and I wondered what the next day was going to bring.

In the morning when I woke up, everyone was quiet except for Little Chipmunk, Cornflower and Night Wind. Most of the medicine women were either in meditation, praying, reading, writing a letter or anything else except talking. I approached Many Names and asked, "Why is everyone so quiet?"

Many Names laughed and said, "The medicine women all over the world honor Mother Earth and Grandmother Moon when the moon is full in the sky."

She paused, took a sip of her coffee and continued, "It is an ancient belief that all medicine women and men must tell the truth when the moon is full in the sky." She took another sip of her coffee and laughed. "Our medicine circle call this twenty-four hour period of time, 'Day of Truth.' You must answer any question during this time with the truth. You must speak the truth or say nothing at all." She sat smiling and finished the rest of her coffee.

Being young and naive, I did not comprehend what Many Names had told me as I walked away. That day, as I prepared the evening's ceremonial fire, I began to asking around for advice about whether I was doing things properly. If I had a question, they motioned me away with their hand or put a finger to their lips instructing me to be quiet. These highly opinionated women were strangely silent. Creepy. After about three hours of this, I had enough and asked Many Names what was going on.

She began to laugh and motioned for me to sit in front of her on the ground. She put the bowl of peas she was shucking aside and folded her hands on her lap. All the other medicine women stopped what they were doing to listen to what Many Names was going to say. Before she spoke, she took a deep breath looked at each one of the women and gave them a nod of acknowledgment. Watching her do this made me think of an owl. She said: "My dear, dear child, did you not listen to what I said to you this morning?"

I looked at her and said, "Yes, I remember." She then asked me to repeat it for her, and I did. Then I said, "I still don't understand. Don't all medicine women speak the truth?"

She smiled at me, patted me on the head and said, "She's so young." She went on to say, "You will understand more tonight. Listen and pay attention." She shooed me away as if I were a dog, so

I looked around all the medicine women either laughing or smiling to themselves.

I was confused now more than ever. I went over to Cornflower to ask to look at my fire circle, and she said, "It looked just fine."

As we walked to the fire circle on the evening of the full moon, the women who had rushed ahead the night before walked in slow motion as if they were dragging their feet. This time there was no wrestling match to sit in front of the talking stick. As we approached the circle, I turned to Many Names and told her I was beginning to understand what she was talking about. The problem I was having was I didn't know how I could listen to the advice of the medicine women. If I have to question everything they tell me and in my mind, what is the truth? Many Names looked at me, gave me a big hug and said, "You're learning."

That evening I sat down in front of the talking stick because I wanted to be the first one to speak. Night Wind said to me, "Before you pick up the stick, you must speak the truth with it tonight," as she patted me on the knee. Cornflower started the ceremony with no arguments from any of the other women. She gave a beautiful blessing and thanked the Great Creator for the new medicine-women-in-training as she pointed to me and Mary. After all the drumming and singing, it was time for the talking stick.

I sat ready to lunge for the talking stick, when I noticed no one else was moving. I started to laugh as what I was told by Many Names finally made sense to me. Many of the medicine women folded their arms and looked down at the ground or fire.

I turned to Cornflower as she spoke to them with a gentle yet firm voice about telling the truth. I reached for the stick and stood up. I asked them to help me become a good medicine woman and to help me follow the medicine path. I thanked them and put the stick back in its special spot and waited for someone to pick it up. They sat there like statues except for Little Chipmunk, Cornflower, and Night Wind. We sat around the fire silently waiting for someone to make a move. It was eerie seeing them so still as if they were frozen in time.

Finally, White Cloud said, "Cornflower, tell us one of your stories."

Cornflower thanked her and got up. I thought I heard a few moans and groans as she picked up the talking stick. She told a beautiful story of how she met her spirit animal, as everyone sat there and listened. When she finished her story, she held out the talking stick to offer it to the other medicine women. You would think she had lit a stick of dynamite in her hand as she put it in front of their faces. One by one, they replied, "I don't remember the story. Give someone else a turn. I've talked enough. Let Cornflower tell another one of her stories."

The evening went on this way until their playfulness got the best of them. They began teasing one another by saying, "I remember the story you told last night, can we hear it again tonight?" Then, they would go on to relate the story the person had told the night before.

This went on for about a half an hour, Many Names got up and said, "Look, I'm giving you women a choice: either we hear another story from Little Chipmunk, Night Wind or Cornflower, or we drum and sing. Your choice." She sat down.

Because they found their stories too boring and lacking in imagination, they always picked drumming and singing. If they did not choose immediately, Little Chipmunk would lecture them about their behavior. As I got up to put another piece of wood on the fire, they said almost in unison, "That's okay, we want to go to bed early tonight."

Little Chipmunk and the other two ladies said, "We don't want them suffering any longer than they have to. Let them go to bed." Everyone left except for Little Chipmunk, Night Wind, Cornflower, Many Names, and a few stragglers. They stayed with me to clean up and tend to the fire. I learned more from the conversation between the medicine women who stayed with me than I had learned all week. The next evening, the medicine women were still subdued and careful about what they said. Even though they tried their best, by the end of the week, things went back to normal.

On the way home on the plane, I asked Many Names why the medicine women acted that way if they knew it was wrong. She took a sip of her coffee, looked out the plane window, took a deep breath, and began to explain.

"Medicine women and men deal with things that are not all black and white. There are many gray areas they deal with that stretch the boundaries of reality. They question everything and everything questions them. The philosophical question was asked, 'If a tree falls in the woods, does it make a sound when no one is there to hear it?' Is man so egocentric that he thinks nothing can happen unless he is there to witness it?"

She paused and sipped more of her coffee. She looked at me and asked, "Are you riding on this plane? Does this plane exist? Maybe if you told someone else they would think you were fantasizing. What proof do you have that you are on this airplane right now?"

She paused again and sipped more of her coffee. "Medicine women and men, in order to heal physical, emotional, or spiritual illness, have to go into the realms of reality that people do not believe exist. When they go into this state of being, they cannot have any doubt in what they are experiencing. For this reason, I want you to write a book on the medicine wheel." I sat and listened.

"This is why the medicine women and men can walk through walls, talk to a person who is dead, and know things of the past and of the future," she told me. "So what if they tell a few tall tales, they're not hurting anyone."

She sat up in her seat and leaned forward to me. "If you want to hear lying that hurts people, go into any court room where they swear on the Bible to tell the truth," she said in a wrathful voice. Before I knew it, we were landing in Boston and on our way home, or were we?

I am going to leave you with my teacher's favorite story.

There was a woman driving her fancy car down the highway. She had just purchased three gallons of wine for her husband from a local vineyard. After driving an hour, she spotted an old Indian woman walking on the side of the road. She looked around and didn't see any other cars, so she stopped.

"Would you like a ride home?" the woman asked.

The Indian woman said, “Yes, thank you, stranger,” as she got into the car.

After driving for about ten minutes, the driver noticed the old Indian woman looking at the bottles of wine. She didn’t want the Indian woman to think she was a drunk, so she said, “I notice you are looking at my wine bottles.”

The Indian woman nodded yes.

“I got them for my husband,” she said, smartly thinking she outsmarted the old woman.

The old Indian woman rubbed her chin and said, “Good trade.”

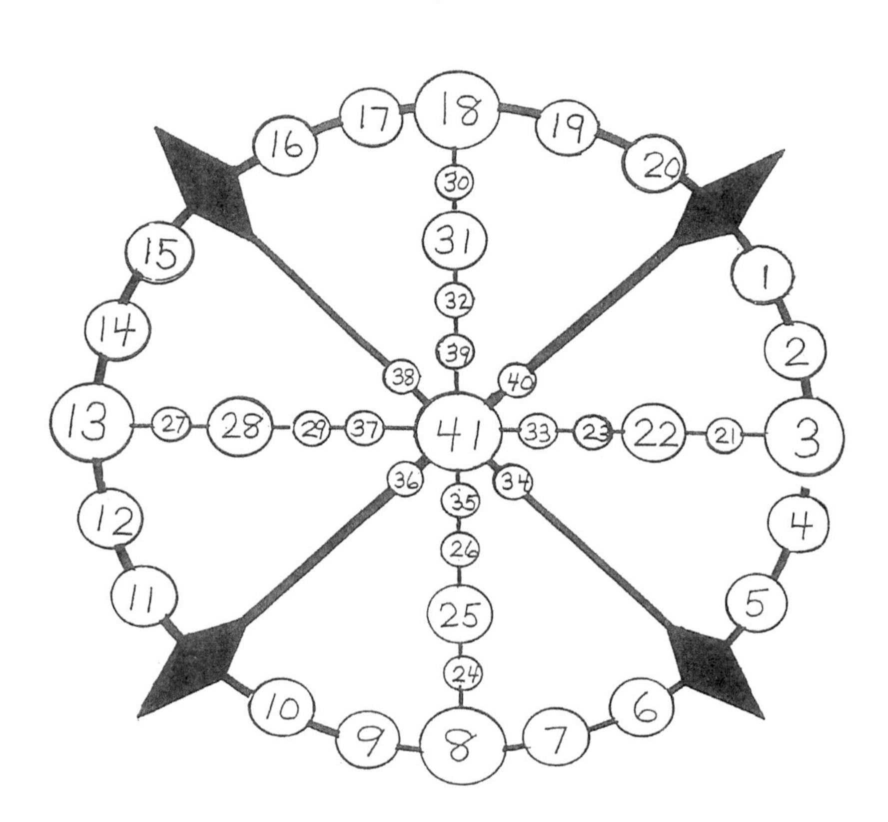

Medicine Wheel

EAST

1. Land: Deer
2. Winged: Turkey
3. Clan: Turtle
4: Water: Beaver
5. Spirit Animal: Red Hawk

SOUTH

6. Land: Lizard
7. Winged: Crow
8. Clan: Deer
9. Water: Dolphin
10. Spirit Animal: Snake

WEST

11. Land: Wolf
12. Winged: Sea gull
13. Clan: Bear
14. Water: Otter
15. Spirit Animal: Bear

NORTH

16. Land: Elk
17. Winged: Raven
18. Clan: Wolf
19. Water: Whale
20. Spirit Animal: Mountain Lion

EAST

21. Season: Spring
21. Time of Day: Sunrise
22. Totem: Eagle
23. Phase of Life: Childhood
23. Emotion: Love / Trust

SOUTH

24. Season: Summer
24. Time of Day: Noon
25. Totem: Coyote
26. Phase of Life: Adolescence
26. Emotions: Hate / Innocence

WEST

27. Season: Autumn
27. Time of Day: Sunset
28. Totem: Bear
29. Phase of Life: Adult
29. Emotions: Happiness / Sorrow

NORTH

30. Season: Winter
30. Time of Day: Night
31. Totem: White Wolf
32. Phase of Life: Elder
32. Emotions: Wisdom / Patience

CENTER CIRCLE

33. Ancestor: Mother Earth
34. Animal Spirit Helper
35. Ancestor: Father Sun
36. Animal Spirit Helper
37. Ancestor: Grandmother Moon
38. Animal Spirit Helper
39. Ancestor: Grandfather Sky
40. Animal Spirit Helper
41. Ancestor: The Great Creator

Practice Work Sheet

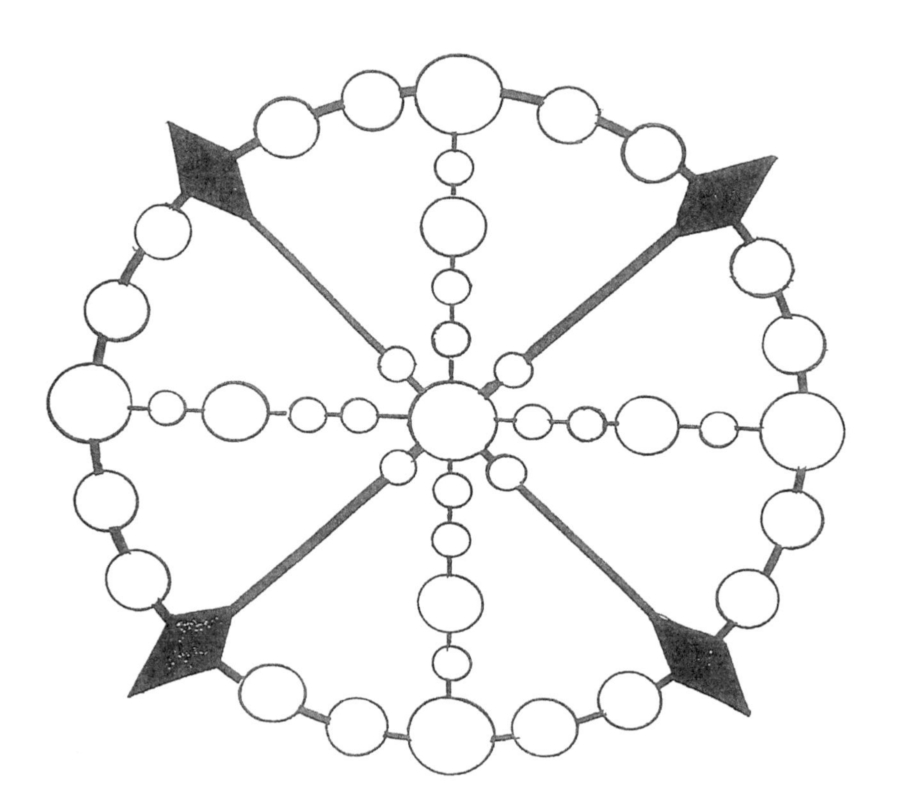

About the Author

Eileen Melanson Hennessey, native name Grandmother Pudding-stone, is a member of Acadiens-Metis-Souriquois in Canada. She is a direct descendant of Chief Henri Membertou of the Mi'Kmaq Nation through her paternal great-grandfather, Freeman Melanson of Nova Scotia. Her paternal great-great-grandmother, Natalie Thibodeau Melanson, is from the Mi'kmaq Nation. They used to live near the Bear River Reservation, Grand Digby, Nova Scotia. She is a direct descendant of Chief Quadequina, Massasoit brother of the Pokanoket, Wampanoag tribe through her paternal great-grand-mother, Katherine Snow Melanson of Massachusetts.

She has a direct line to the Mayflower Hopkins through Katherine Snow Melanson. When the Mayflower came to shore in the new world, Eileen's ancestors were on the ship and the people on the shore looking at each other. They ended up marrying each other. Eileen and her family is the end result.

Her ancestors, Brigadier General, and later Deputy Governor, William West and Capt. Jacob Fuller served in the Revolutionary War. She had family fighting on the British side. Her ancestor was the Honorable Philip Sherman and his wife, Sarah Odding. He was the first treasurer of Rhode Island. He was a slave owner, trader, and very good friends with the DeWolfe and Brown family of Rhode Island. He was thrown out of Massachusetts with Roger Williams to help start the Providence Plantations.

When her great-grandfather Freeman came down from Nova Scotia to Massachusetts, he brought with him his traditions and love for the Mi'kmaq Nation. It is no surprise he fell in love with Kate who carried on her native traditions as well. Eileen's grandfather Henri would always make them laugh at his stories.

You have a good chance of finding Eileen singing native songs and playing her guitar at Powwows in Connecticut, Massachusetts, Maine, New Hampshire, New York, Rhode Island, and Vermont.

She is often invited to sing and speak at colleges, universities and private events.

If you need to contact her, you can private message her on Facebook: Eileen Grandmother Puddingstone Hennessey.

CPSIA information can be obtained
at www.ICGtesting.com
Printed in the USA
FFHW022216150319
51094340-56521FF

9 781644 628096